SLIDING INTO HOME

A Novel By

Nina Vincent

For TJ...

Thank you for helping me expand beyond places of comfort and knowing, and for demanding that I step out of the boxes that kept my world small. You are my Flip, my Kaylee, and my Zorba.

For Eli...

Thank you for your steady support and belief in me as a writer. You are my teacher and my friend.

Acknowledgements

To Kasey, Rina, and Sharon—the Pelicans:

Thank you for your guidance and friendship. Our writers' circle made this an adventure and a joy.

PART I

Life is like a baseball game. You can be ahead by a lot in the first few innings. But if the bases are loaded, it only takes one solid hit to turn the game around. That's how it was for my family.

CHAPTER ONE

Sundays, Dad and I go to the park to play ball. I pitch, he catches.

I don't play pitcher on my school team, but I still like practicing. You never know, one day my coach might holler to me in left field: "Hey Simpson – we're in a pinch. Come take the mound and show us what you've got." I know it's not likely, but one can always hope.

The coach calls me "Simpson." My name is Flip. Flip Simpson.

I was Felipe when I came home to San Francisco from Guatemala, until my little sister Kaylee came along. When she started talking, her twisted little tongue couldn't wrap itself around the word Felipe. It strangled the *e*'s right out of my name. That's where "Flip" came from. It stuck.

We live in the lower half of Noe Valley, on 24th street near the Mission. If you walk up 24th street, the weather gets colder, and the neighborhood begins to change. Dad calls the Mission, "San Francisco's south of the border."

That works for me, since I look like I'm from south of the border. Mom says my skin is the color of a strong cup of tea. I think it's more like the color of a sweet bar of chocolate.

My last pitch of the day is a doozy. Dad whistles when it hits his glove, then he whips it off and blows on his hand. That's his way of letting me know it came in fast and hard.

"If you keep that ball coming in at two hundred miles an hour, your coach is going to beg you to pitch." He doesn't put his glove back on, which means practice is over.

"Yeah right, Dad, two hundred miles an hour? Has anyone ever pitched over a hundred miles an hour?" I move off my throne on the mound and meet Dad in the middle.

"Yep, I just read about a Reds pitcher who threw one in at a hundred and five miles an hour!"

"Whoa. That's a fast ball!"

Dad's smile slides further up one side of his face than the other. It makes his teeth look shorter on one side. The blue of his eyes disappears when his smile is big.

I ask Dad as we pull into the driveway if he and Mom are going out to celebrate her birthday tonight. Mom loves birthdays.

"No, actually we're not." There's no crooked smile. His teeth disappear behind his closed lips. His blue eyes are wide open.

I follow Dad into the house, pulling the short hairs around my ears until it hurts. Kaylee and Mom are in the kitchen.

"I'm going to go change," Dad says. He scrapes his sneakers off and throws them in the closet. "I'll see you in a bit, buddy."

I head for the laughter in the kitchen. The collection of family in frames along the wall calls to me as I walk by. I stop in front of the first photos taken of me the day I came home from Guatemala twelve years ago. All four of my front teeth peek out from a hill of gums in my wide open mouth. My skin is lighter in those early photos. The orphanage *niñeras* had me dressed in a pair of colorful pants, a white shirt, and a crocheted hat.

I know this is a picture of me, but whenever I look at it I feel as if I'm staring at a stranger.

The next photo is of Kaylee right after she was born. She fits so perfectly in my mother's arms. In the photo I look down at my baby sister, my two-year-old stubby fingers rest on her bald head. Mom's eyes are glued to her new baby girl. My body leans in so close to the two of them it looks like I may fall into Mom's lap.

I walk away from that happy little family scene but not before I notice that the last family photo is the one we took of our trip to Yosemite almost two years ago.

Mom appears at the end of the hall. Her apron is covered in chocolate handprints. "Hey, I thought I heard you come in. Do you want to help Kaylee in the kitchen? She's icing the cake and is ready to lick the bowl – your timing is perfect!"

Mom walks towards me. Her brown hair is tied in a knot on the back of her head. Strands like muddy shoelaces dangle alongside her sandy tanned face.

"Mmm, sounds great, Mom. Dad's taking a shower." I watch her face carefully as she answers.

"Good. I'll start dinner as soon as the cake is out of the oven. How was baseball?"

"Great. I pitched all strikes!"

"That's my boy." She squeezes my shoulder as she walks by.

I hope Kaylee hasn't already cleaned the bowl with her quick little licking fingers.

I stop and poke my head into the kitchen. Her back is to me and what's left of the icing bowl is on the table. I creep in quietly and grab the bowl, ducking around the corner before she sees me. Seconds later I hear Kaylee say, "Hey, what? Where?" and then silence.

I can't help it. I have to see her face. I look around the corner just as she's walking out of the kitchen.

"Arghhh," she squeals.

"Ha!" I blast back.

She bursts out laughing. "Oh my god, Flip, you scared the boogers out of me. You took the icing, I couldn't find it..."

I take my finger and sweep it around the chocolate-covered inside of the bowl, waving it in Kaylee's face before popping it in my mouth. "Mmmmm, that is sooooo goooood."

She reaches out to dip her fingers in the silky chocolate. I shift so my body blocks her and hug the bowl tighter.

4

"Flip! You have to share that with me. I was the one who made the cake, you know. You don't get to walk in and eat all the good stuff!"

I'm not in the mood to torture her today so I swing the bowl around. "Here, have a lick, then let's go into the kitchen and finish it off."

Her overalls are covered in white flour and icing. "Jeesh, you look like a creative arts project. You're covered in Mom's birthday cake!"

Kaylee looks down the front of herself and shrugs. "I don't care," she says, although she sounds as if she does.

I take a few more swipes around the inside of the bowl and then get up from the table. "That's it for me," I say and head out of the kitchen. When I look back, I see Kaylee watching me. Her face looks sad, as if she wishes I would stay.

Upstairs I hear them. My foot stops in midair.

"*I'm sorry*," my dad says, sounding more angry than sorry. "I didn't think you *wanted* to go out for your birthday. I would have been happy to go out if that's what you wanted."

"I shouldn't have to *tell* you that I want to go out, Fenton. It's my birthday. You could have planned something in advance rather than waiting for me to ask."

Why does Mom have to yell at him all the time? My father seems to be one big disappointment to my mother. I wish she'd just leave him alone.

I tiptoe up the stairs and down the hall, closing my bedroom door quietly behind me. I stand in the middle of my room, Jose Canseco and a few of my other favorite players look down from their places on the ceiling and walls. I know what they're thinking, "Trouble is coming..."

5

I shake my head and grab a handful of my hair. I tug it hard. The pain makes my eyes water. The room is quiet except for the rumble of angry voices down the hall.

#

"Hey Flip, slow down! When did you get motor-controlled legs?" Kaylee does a skip and a hop trying to catch up to me. She looks like a stumbling kangaroo. I wish she'd leave me alone. I'm trying to figure things out.

I know Mom and Dad are mad at each other, but at dinner last night they seemed so normal, even happy to be celebrating her birthday.

"Flip! What's your hurry?" Kaylee whines.

"I don't get it." I stop for a second so she can catch up. I don't want her to have a freaking heart attack on the way to school. When she's standing close enough that I could yank on her braid, I move again.

"I'm the one with the short legs, but you're the one who's always lagging behind. How come?" I hate my short legs. Everyone else in my family has long wiry legs. Mine are stubby and thick.

"Who said short legs are slow legs? You're faster than me right now, that's all."

"Right now and always." I'm not having as much fun teasing Kaylee as I normally do. There's heaviness in my gut today that I can't shake.

Jerry stands at the corner waiting for us. His neon orange pinny makes him look like one of those cones that block a parking space. His grey hair is straight as straw and sticks out the sides of his crossing guard cap. He looks like a scarecrow.

"Goooood morning, kids." Jerry stretches the word "good" like a rubber band and snaps "morning" out like a whip.

"Hey, Jerry," Kaylee calls out to him. Jerry has been standing on this same corner since we were in kindergarten. He's here every day whether it's drippy cold rainy or blazing hot sunny.

Jerry smiles. His huge wrinkled hand speckled with brown spots pats Kaylee on the head.

"Hello, Kaylee – Kaylaaa. How's my *over-all* fantastic little spark plug doing this fine morning?"

Jerry's making a comment on Kaylee's clothes. She wears overalls every day of the year, no matter what. It's her thing. She got her first pair of overalls (the white ones with all the pockets) when she was five. Everyone told her how cute she looked; my parents, the librarian at school, and Jerry, of course. I think he called her "the little carpenter girl." He told her what the loops and pockets were for. All the attention made her feel special, so she started wearing that same pair of overalls every single day. They turned a kind of funky grey; it drove Mom crazy. Kaylee begged her to buy more. Eventually Mom gave in, and that started her collection of overalls.

She wears them like a second skin.

Jerry's always thinking of funny names for Kaylee. Some days she's a "firecracker" or a "hot tamale." Other days, she's something softer and less snappy like a "buttered bun," or a "cotton candy kid." But this morning she's a "spark plug."

"I'm good, Jerry. Isn't a spark plug something you find in a car?"

Jerry moves into the center of the road with his huge red stop sign. He pushes the sign out with such force that no car would ever dream of ignoring it.

He nods towards Kaylee. "Yep, you got it. It's the spark that makes that engine purr."

Jerry motions for us to come into the crosswalk. "And what about you, Mr. Flip? What are we batting these days?"

"I'm batting 400," I tell him. Batting 400 is almost impossible.

"Nothing I wouldn't have expected," he says with a wink and a smack on the back. "Now go bat a thousand in math and English and you'll be a real star."

We make it to the other side of the road and wave goodbye.

"See you tomorrow," Kaylee calls out.

"Yep, and the day after that as well," Jerry calls back. "I'll see you until summer sweeps you away and brings you back in September."

He turns and heads back to the other side of the street to ferry the next group of kids crossing the city's river of cars.

My stomach drops and I sink to the basement. I have no idea why. What Jerry just said hit an alarm inside of me. My mind doubles back to where it was before when I hear the horn blast. I cover my ears and Kaylee shrieks. I look back to see Jerry on the ground, his orange pinny up around his ears. A huge truck has blown through the cross walk and speeds down the road. I run back into the crosswalk.

"Jerry, are you okay?" He grabs my arm and pulls himself up.

"He almost ran me down. That's the first time in twenty years anyone has ignored that stop sign. You kids could've been killed." He squeezes my shoulder hard, then bends to pick up the stop sign. His crossing guard hat falls off as he does. I'm surprised to see that the top of his head is bald. His scarecrow hair looks so thin and fragile.

"Okay, Flip, you get on to school now. You'll be late."

I don't want to leave him.

"Hey, Flip," a voice calls out. I turn to see several of my teammates rushing to meet me.

Jerry covers the bald spot with his hat and leads us across the street. Kaylee stands on the side of the road waiting for me.

"Oh my god, Flip, that guy almost killed Jerry."

"Did you see how bald he is?" Andrew says. "All these years and I never knew the guy had no hair under that hat."

I wish Andrew would shut up. There's too much noise and chaos in my head.

CHAPTER TWO

"No, that's not what I'm saying at all! Do you even listen to me, or do you just listen to what you want to hear?"

I look at Kaylee over our game of Battleship. "Really?" she says. "Again? All they seem to do these days is scream at each other."

"H-4," I say, trying to ignore Kaylee.

Kaylee thumps her hand against her leg. "You found my little one again. Argh, how come you always find that one first?"

I shrug and wink at her 'cause I know she hates when I do.

"Fine, I'm going out. I'll be back late – don't hold dinner for me," I hear Dad yell from the living room.

"Oh great, Fenton, how is that going to help if every time we have a disagreement you just leave?"

"I'm taking a time out." The front door slams and then the dreaded silence that comes after the yelling.

Kaylee shifts in her spot on the floor and fiddles with the shoulder strap of her striped overalls. I know she's about to say something stupid.

"I hate when they fight like this. I'm so afraid…"

I slam the lid down on my ships. The red and white pegs rain down onto the floor. Her stupid chatter makes everything worse.

"I don't want to play anymore," I say.

"Flip," Kaylee yells at me.

I leave. She can pick up the mess herself. I don't care.

#

On Saturday, Kaylee and I come home from the Mission Dolores Park. Our school is only a few blocks from there. Dolores Park is also near the Castro, and the Castro's famous. It's one of the best known gay neighborhoods around. Mom says the Castro is a rainbow of diversity and that we're lucky to live in a city that celebrates all kinds of people.

I love Dolores Park on the weekends. There's always a game of kickball or basketball going on. Kaylee and her friends like to play tag or hang out in the playground.

We have to leave the park early today. A weird wind came up suddenly, blowing dirt and debris into our eyes. Many kids decide to go home.

Kaylee talks a mile a minute as we climb our front door steps, "You should have seen it, Flip. Sandra was just inches away from Inez and then she tripped and landed in the little kids' sandbox. It was so funny."

I have to push hard against the wind to close the door behind us. "Sounds like Sandra needs to wear her glasses when she plays tag."

"Glasses? Sandra doesn't wear glasses." I roll my eyes and throw my jacket on the stool by the hallway closet. Kale turns towards me and starts laughing, "Your hair looks like a wind-whipped Mohawk."

I smile as I pat the top of my head. I feel the spikes of hair prickle the palm of my hand, and then I feel something else. The air is thick.

Mom and Dad are sitting in the front room. Mom's red t-shirt hangs over her blue jeans like a curtain. Dad sits across the room from her in the big brown armchair.

The den is a small room. My parents are sitting miles apart.

"Hey Mom, hey Dad, you should've seen how many kids were in the park today. It was like the entire school showed up on a Saturday," Kaylee babbles on.

"Hey kids." There's almost no sound behind Mom's words. Only air.

"Hey, Flip, buddy, come on in here for a minute – both of you. Your mom and I want to talk to you."

My dad's voice has a hook on the end. It tries to draw us into the den. I don't move. I can't. Kaylee walks around me and into the room. She hesitates for a second and then sits next to Mom.

"Flip, honey, come sit down please." Mom's words have filled themselves up with sound again.

"No!" I will not go into that room.

Kaylee's body shifts on the couch. Dad slumps back in his chair and Mom puts her hand lightly on Kaylee's leg. She looks at my father and waits to see if he is going to speak. When he doesn't, she looks at Kaylee.

"Kids, your father and I have decided we're going to separate for a while."

The minute the words are out of her mouth something sharp shoots through my body, from my feet all the way to the top of my head. I'm lifted into the air and am running up the stairs to my room. I slam my door so hard I'm certain it must be cracked down the middle.

I can't think. My brain is a block of ice. I curl up on my bed and put my head between my knees and squeeze. I hear myself crying but it feels like I'm not a part of that. Someone else is doing the crying inside of me. I don't know how long it is before I hear the knock on my door.

"*Go away!*" I scream. I don't think the words actually find their way out of my mouth.

There's another knock on the door. When it opens, I raise my head long enough to see my dad edge into the room. He closes the door behind him.

I bury my head back between my knees.

"Hey, can we talk?" His voice tiptoes in behind him as he moves onto the bed beside me.

His hand is on my back. My muscles bundle and tighten. "I'm sorry, Flip. I'm just so sorry."

"Why, Dad?"

"Your mother and I have tried so hard to make it work. We can't live together. We don't love each other that way anymore."

"What does that even mean? How do you decide one day that you don't love someone, or that you don't want to live together anymore?"

I squeeze my head between my knees, harder.

I feel my dad's hand resting on my back. It doesn't feel like a hand anymore. It feels like dressing on a wound.

#

"That's the worst news ever," Kaylee's friend Shawna wails on the other end of the phone. "Why would they move out of the city, in the middle of the school year?"

"My parents are splitting up," Kaylee tells her friend.

There's a noticeable silence before Shawna says, "Oh wow, that's a bummer."

Then Kaylee says something really stupid. "Yeah, but who knows, maybe it's just temporary." She sweeps the truth under a carpet of fantasies.

"Well, you'll be back to visit, and you'll always be my best friend no matter what," Shawna promises.

I know this because I am listening to their conversation on the upstairs phone. I didn't plan to. I started to hang up when Kaylee got on the line, but she launched into my parents' story and I got curious. I don't think Kaylee even knows what's true anymore. I hear her tell a new story every day.

"Yeah, I know it really sucks. My dad is relocating – there's a big job for him in Marin and the commute is just too much. But we'll be back to visit lots."

#

"It's only three weeks of class – I'm not going to get anything done anyways!" I scream.

I can't believe my mother thinks that saying goodbye to my friends and teachers will be a good way to "experience closure."

"He doesn't want the reality of our leaving to be confirmed by 'goodbye' day in and day out. Let's just let it go, Sheila," my father argues with her when she tries to convince him to make me go to school. In the end, Mom wins. She always does.

And now I'm forced to face the telling, and the truth.

I walk through the hallways of my school as if I just arrived and I'm seeing them for the first time. They no longer belong to me. Everyone I see becomes either a person I will or will not tell.

My teammates can't believe it when I tell them.

"Dude, you can't leave. We have the finals coming up in May. How are we going to win without you?" Tyson pulls his cap off his head and slaps it against his thigh.

"No way, Flip. That's just wrong. We've been playing ball together since second grade, man. Just tell your parents you're not going. You can come live at my house." Kenny pushes his long stringy hair out of his eyes, tucking it under his cap while shaking his head at the same time. "Really, Flip, you can't move."

I feel like screaming at them all. They make it sound like I have a choice. I shake my head and try to explain, "I know, but the problem is – I am. We only have three weeks left 'til moving day and there's nothing I can do about it."

Telling my coach is the worst.

"My family is moving." I stare down at my running shoes for the longest time, and then out the window. "I'm leaving soon."

Coach Dave tugs at the whistle around his neck, something he does all the time during practice even though he never uses it.

"Well, Simpson, I don't think I need to tell you how much you'll be missed here. You've been such an important and valuable player for the school. Wherever you go next – they'll be darn lucky to have you on the team."

I nod and try to swallow but my throat is choking itself, and all I can do is breathe.

"We've got you for a little time more, right?"

"Yes, sir. We leave in three weeks, at spring break."

I barely recognize my voice. It's tight and squeaky. I wonder if the coach notices. I walk out of his office, out of the gym, and out of my school. My eyes burn. I run through the park, down the sidewalks past stores I've known my whole life, to the home I will no longer come back to at the end of school each day.

I spend the weekend packing. I pull the posters that my dad and I have collected over the years off the walls. Each time another baseball player comes down it feels like I've lost a friend. I fold years of my life into little squares and stuff them into cardboard boxes.

The last weeks of school are torture. When I pass my friends in the hall, the best I can give them is a nod. I used to hang out at my locker talking with friends about projects or baseball. Now I don't want to talk. I don't want to be reminded of all that I'm leaving behind. So, I just stand at my locker alone and walk to my classes as quickly as I can. I guess my friends are confused by how I'm acting because they've stopped asking me about class assignments or when I'm leaving.

Coming home after school is like a punishment. I can't be in the same room with my parents.

"Flip, why don't you come on into the kitchen and I'll make you a snack." Mom pretends that everything is sweet and normal. I'm not going to play her happy family game.

Dad knows better. Sometimes he'll give me a squeeze on the shoulder. I think he's too sad to speak too.

When I get home from school, I go to my bedroom and close the door. I sit on my floor with the dust balls and dirty socks and stare out at nothing. I can't tell you why, but the numbness inside almost feels good – like going on vacation.

After a while, my mother knocks on the door. "Flip, dinner's ready. Come downstairs and wash up."

I can't. I don't want to sit around the kitchen table, all together. So I don't. I stretch out on the bare floor.

I used to have a Jose Canseco poster on the ceiling above my bed. Now there are four ripped corners still stuck under the tape.

I stare at the empty ceiling. And that's where I am later when my dad knocks on the door. "Hey buddy, can I come in?"

I feel a tug deep inside. I want to see my dad, to feel him next to me. But I want to punish him more.

He knocks a bit more loudly. "Felipe. I'd like to come in."

I can't refuse my dad. "Yeah," I tell him, hating myself for being weak.

My dad is the kind of man you read about in story books. He's super good looking. His brown hair sweeps down over his forehead. He flips it back out of his eyes like a movie star. But he doesn't have the pretty face of an actor. He's rugged. His skin is caramel candy tan in the summer months, and beluga whale white in the winter.

He works in construction, so he's super strong. He could still lift me over his head and spin me around in the air when I was eight or nine. He's also an athlete. He taught me how to play baseball, throw a football, ride my bike.

He taught me everything I know. And he's been here with me at the beginning and the end of every day.

When I think that he won't be any more I feel like I'm falling off a cliff, but there's no ground waiting at the bottom for me to hit. The falling never ends.

"Hey buddy, we'd really like you to come down and have dinner with us. You can't stay up here by yourself forever."

"Yeah I can, Dad."

He sits on my bed and looks down at me on the floor. His eyes follow the trail of poster corners still taped to the wall. They circle the room and then land on me again.

"It's lonely in here without them, isn't it?"

I nod.

After a few minutes, Dad gets up. He bends down and rubs the top of my head.

"I love you, Flip." He closes the door behind him.

The next night, Mom sends Kaylee up to get me for dinner.

"Flip, Mom says it's dinnertime." Kaylee doesn't knock on the door. She stands outside it. I can tell by the way her voice squeezes into the room that she has her face squished up against the crack. Her breath slips through the tiny space between the closed door and the wall. I listen hard, holding my breath. I let it out quietly so she doesn't hear.

"Whatever," she says. Her footsteps move away from my door.

My parents begin to argue about whether I should have to eat dinner with them. I haven't come down for dinner in four days. It would be weird to show up at the dinner table now, even if I wanted to.

Kaylee walks beside me on the way to school every morning without a word. I can tell she wants to talk to me, but I think she's afraid to. My silence has become a cloak that separates me from my family.

A week before we move, Jerry notices Kaylee dragging along beside me on the way to school. "Hey my little cherry blossom – why so down?"

"We have to move, Jerry."

"Move? Huh. Well that's a curve ball I never expected."

Jerry looks at me but I don't want him to see the tears that burn the rims of my eyes. I put my head down and walk across the street.

"Well, you two have the best day you can," Jerry says as we walk past. His body with its neon orange vest is as familiar to me as the streetlight and the stationary store.

"Mom says our new house is right near a little beach." Kaylee's overalls are loose around her belly and even though they're supposed to be shorts they hang below her knees. This makes me smile. As soon as Kaylee sees the smile, she starts talking more.

"And she says the school sits up on a hill and you can see the sailboats in the harbor from the classroom."

"Cool," I say, because I don't want to freeze Kaylee out of my life.

Later at home, Kaylee knocks on my door and asks to come in. I'm on the floor leaning against my bed, staring at the wall. Kaylee sits beside me. She doesn't say anything. She stares at the wall with me. I want to laugh it feels so good to have her here.

Mom calls to us from downstairs. "Kaylee, Flip, dinner is ready."

Kaylee looks over at me.

"You go," I tell her.

She shakes her head no. "I'm staying here with you."

"You don't have to," I tell her. "You should go eat dinner."

"Not unless you do." She crosses her arms over her chest as though she is three years old and refusing to take a bath.

"Ok then," I say and turn back to the wall.

It feels different now, like a room has opened up inside of me and Kaylee has come in.

When I was small, Mom and Dad tell me I had such horrible separation anxiety that if they left a room and I couldn't see them I would have convulsive fits.

They say I was so out of my mind that I wouldn't even get up and try to find them, I'd just roll around on the floor screaming their names. When one of them would come back into the room, I would attach myself to their legs or bodies and eventually they would have to peel me off.

I don't really remember that, but when they tell me, I can *feel* it somewhere deep down inside. It's like someone turned a switch onto the fast forward setting inside my body. Everything races inside, and I get this buzzing in my ears, sort of like a swarm of bees.

When I think of a life without my father in it, I am swallowed by the buzzing.

#

We're moving in just a few days now. Everything we own is in boxes. The house echoes with its emptiness.

It doesn't feel real to me.

Kaylee sits next to me in my room and starts to talk. Most of the time she sits quietly. Sometimes she brings a book or one of her stupid girly magazines in to read. Today she's thinking out loud. "Have you noticed how quiet it's been around here lately? Mom and Dad haven't been fighting almost at all."

I can tell this nags at her in a hopeful sort of way. She wants to believe that maybe they're changing their minds. Maybe they've found a way to make it work after all.

I feel grateful Kaylee is here in my room some days. I've started going down to have dinner again because I couldn't sit up here and make her miss dinner every night.

But this is too much. I can't stand the way she tries to live in this fantasy world, weaving her little blanket of lies and wrapping it around her so that she can feel all safe and warm.

"They're not yelling at each other anymore doesn't mean they're not separating. What's wrong with you? Don't you get it? They're not getting back together. Not now, not ever. Just because you tell all your little friends that we're moving because Dad got a new job doesn't make it true."

I'm screaming at her. She flinches.

"My god, okay! Don't get so mad at me."

My bedroom door is open. I look past her at all the boxes stacked in the hallway, at the undeniable reality of what's happening and I want to scream. I jump up from the floor and head out the door. I can't do what she does. It seems like so much work the way she pretends that none of this is real.

I want to get it over with now. I want us to move so I can stop waiting for the worst day of my life to happen. The weird thing is that most of the time I don't feel anything inside.

The electricity has been turned off. The lights are out, and everything inside of me has gone dead.

#

"Alright, I think that's it." Dad is helping us move into Mom's house. He puts the last box down in the corner of my new room.

The walls of my room are different colors; muddy sky blue on one side, and dirty gold brown on the other. My window looks out onto the front of the house. The U-Haul truck parked on the road is empty.

My bed frame is the last thing to come out of it. Dad and I put it together and throw my sheets stuffed into a pillowcase on the bed.

"Ya wanna make it up?" He points to the sheets.

I shrug and sit on the bed. He sits down beside me.

"Are you going back to the city tonight?" I can't look at him, so I focus on a dark brown spot that looks like an old dried up blood stain on the wood floor.

"Yes. I'll be in the city for a few more weeks until my apartment is available. You and Kale will be coming in to see me on the weekends this month, then we'll switch to every other weekend and Wednesday nights."

"I know, Dad, I do have a memory you know." I don't know how many times he has gone over the moving plan. It doesn't turn into good news just because he keeps telling it to me. It's the same bad story every time.

He stands up. "Come on, Flip, let's make the bed. You can unpack the boxes tomorrow if you like. We've done enough for one day."

I grab the pillowcase with my sheets in it and yank them out hard.

Kaylee is in her room unpacking her boxes. She and I have bedrooms on the first floor in this house. Mom's room is upstairs, separated from ours by a distance that feels like it's growing.

The kitchen is much smaller than the one we have in the city, and the den is about the size of a closet. The colors are funky too. Who paints one wall dark red and another gold? It looks like an unfinished art project to me. Mom says she loves the way each room is painted a different color but I miss the plain white walls of our place in the city.

I hear Kaylee talking to my dad. "I really like my new room. It gets more sun than the one in the city and I can see the birds in the little tree outside my window."

I peek in to see how she's placed her bed so she can look out the window when she sits up. Her room is a bright yellow on three walls, and then a darker blue on the fourth.

"Hey Kale bug – I'm going to take off now, sweetheart. I'll stop by tomorrow to help you guys unpack some more."

Kaylee pops her head out of the last unpacked box. "Can't you stay for dinner?"

"Not tonight. I have to get the U-Haul truck back to the city."

Kaylee looks away from our dad and clenches her fist and then quickly crosses the room and falls into his arms weeping. Dad gives her a long hug. He walks past me standing in the doorway and gives my shoulder a squeeze. Then he leaves.

I want to run after him, to grab his leg and wrap myself around it so he can't get out the door.

The front door clicks as it closes behind him.

Starting right now, our father no longer lives in the same house with us.

CHAPTER THREE

Moving day is over. Boxes line the walls and are stacked like high rises in the corners of each room. Six large boxes with books, posters, trophies, clothing, games, and baseball cards sit in the corner of my room in two towers, three stories high.

I empty the boxes of clothing for obvious reasons. I'm not ready to put the rest of this new life on the walls and shelves of my room.

When I lay my head on the pillow to sleep, all I can think about is my dad, home alone in the city without us.

In the morning, the sun comes through the naked windows like a highway of light that crosses the foot of my bed and crashes into the wall.

The sounds here are different than at home in the city. It's early, but by now the 24th Street bus would have passed my bedroom window, its weight pushing loudly against the brakes that keep it from blasting down the hill like a rolling boulder.

That bus was the first alarm of many in my city life. I learned to sleep through almost all of them. The fire trucks and ambulances were the only alarms that pierced through the soundproof canvas of my sleep, probably because there was no predictability to them.

The silence of this place is louder than the ambulance sirens. It's one long, never-ending stream of nothingness that pushes up against my eardrums until they hurt.

I listen for Mom in the kitchen, or the sound of the water as it comes through the loud pipes in the walls, letting me know that as soon as she's finished with her shower, she'll be in to wake me up.

Not today. Today Mom is upstairs in her room by herself because she and Dad wanted it that way.

I hate this place. I hate this place. I hate this place.

#

Dad arrives midday. Mom has finished unpacking her books. I hate the fact that her books fit perfectly on the built-into-the-wall bookshelves, each bookish space is taken by titles of books I'd never even noticed before. *The House of Spirits*, by Isabel Allende. *Zorba the Greek*, by Nikos Katzanzakis and *The Grapes of Wrath*, by John Steinbeck. Okay, I've heard of that one. But the rest of them, Alice Walker, Deepok Choprah, Milan Kundera – who are these people?

I'm holding *Zorba the Greek* when Dad's pick-up pulls into the driveway. Mom is upstairs putting away the bathroom towels and linens. Kaylee is beautifying her room. Last I looked, she was putting her six gazillion glass animals back onto their field of green on top of her dresser. She likes her room here better than the one in the city. That makes me crazy inside. I need her to hate this as much as I do.

There's a knock on the front door. Dad *knocked* on the front door! At least he doesn't stand outside waiting for someone to answer the door. He sticks his head in and sees me coming to let him in.

"Oh, hey champ."

"Dad, why are you knocking on the door?"

"I don't know, son. It just seemed like the right thing to do. It's a little weird though, isn't it?"

"No, Dad. It's not *a little* weird, it's ridiculous. Please, don't knock on the door – you're not some salesman coming to the house."

"Hi, Fenton," Mom stands at the top of the stairs. "No need to knock. Just give a holler when you come in so we know who it is."

Mom's tone is softer. There's sadness in her steps as she comes down the stairs. Each foot sits a bit longer than it should before moving on to the next step.

"I was just finishing in the linen closet. Do you think you could help me with some of the heavier stuff in the den? I'd like to get the TV room set up for the kids."

"Yeah. Of course." Dad looks away from Mom as if it hurt him to hear her request. He notices the book in my hand.

"*Zorba!* Now there's an old friend. I love Zorba. Are you reading it?"

"This? No way. I was just looking at some of the books on the shelves. I've never noticed them before."

"There are some really good ones there. You ought to read this one though. Zorba's one in a million."

"You can take that if you like," Mom says, standing beside us now. "There are probably a few more in there that you might like to keep. I didn't sort them when I packed."

"Thanks," Dad says. "I'll wait until I get settled in my place. Flip, you keep that one. It's a classic."

I hold the book to my chest.

Kaylee hears Dad and comes out of her room. "Dad, come see my room. It looks great. Once I get the curtains up it'll be totally finished."

"I just found the box with the curtains for both your rooms," Mom says. "I'll help you hang them later."

"You want to come see it?" Kaylee wraps her arms around Dad's skinny waist. His arm crosses her shoulder as he pulls her in closer. He kisses the top of her head.

"Sure, honey. Let me just help your mom move some of the furniture in the den, then I'd love to see what you two have done in your new rooms."

"I'm not done unpacking," I say. "I'll show it to you when I'm finished. I'm not in the mood to do it now."

Mom and Dad look at one another. They have the same look they did when I refused to come out of my room, or talk to anyone. I hate that look.

"Ok, son. How 'bout you come help me move some of this furniture with your mom?"

"Fine," I say. I take *Zorba the Greek* with me into the den. I don't want to lose track of him.

#

Kaylee and I decide to check out the neighborhood.

The houses that line the streets of Sausalito seem small compared to the ones in the city. There aren't as many dramatic rooftops, or fancy trims painted eggplant purple, or baby blue. The houseboats are cool, though. And I like being so close to the water. You can see Alcatraz and San Francisco from town.

There are tons of trees wearing spring's new green leaves along their branches. And blue sky everywhere. I never noticed so much blue sky when I was in the city. I like the coolness of the green grass in front of our house. I like the way it feels on my bare feet. I can't remember going outside in bare feet in the city. That's not something you do.

There is so much white in this town, too. White people everywhere. I haven't seen one single brown person in the streets where we live. Mom says the school we're going to is very diverse.

"Kids from Marin City, San Rafael, and even some from San Francisco come to this school."

That's nice. But I still feel a bit like a coffee stain on a white tile floor when Kaylee and I walk through town.

Kaylee is my new sidekick. We only have one another.

"Where do you want to go today?" She'll ask me over breakfast.

"Let's go to town."

"Okay."

She's happy to do whatever I say. I don't mind that. But I miss my friends in the city. I can't talk baseball with Kaylee, or practice my hitting. We tried that one day in the park by the library. I was ready to quit after ten minutes of watching her chase the balls I hit.

29

Kaylee stood in left field and my line drive went right, so she stood in right field. The dang ball went left. Kaylee darted left and right for more hits than I would have.

When my last pop fly flew to left field, Kaylee watched from the right. She turned and walked off the field, towards the library, and said, "As soon as I grow four legs and a tail I'll go get that ball."

I should've saved batting practice for Dad.

"Are you nervous about school?" she asks a few days before spring break ends.

"I don't know," I lie. The truth is, I am. But I'm also ready to do something other than hang out with my sister every single day.

"I am," she says. Nervous wobbles out of her mouth. "What if no one likes me? Or I don't like anyone here? I've never had to make new friends before. I don't even know how to do that."

I know exactly what she means. I never considered what it would be like to have to make new friends. How does one "make" a friend? My friends in San Francisco were just there, since kindergarten. Sure, new kids came, and some friends left, but I always had my place among them.

"It'll be fine," I say. I don't know if I believe it, though.

#

"Let's go explore down by the water again." I look up from behind the box of Cheerios which has become our new staple food on the weekends when Mom leaves for work early.

"Ok. I wanna go see the houseboats."

"Okay, fine." I like hanging out around the waterfront. There's always something new to see.

The tide is low when we get there. The air is a mixture of salty seaweed and sewage sludge. I like it. Kaylee and I start at the fancy part of the waterfront, closer to town. The huge, mostly white sailboats with their mostly white owners scrub their decks and get ready for a day on the water. Their boats have names like *Princess II* and *Ana Maria. Black Beauty* stands out among the boats along its dock. Its raven black with shiny gold-painted trim, outlined in white is exactly what its name says it is. I'd like to have a sail on that boat.

We continue along the maze of docks calling out the names of the boats we like: *Shaggy Dog, Happy Endings, Red Baron.*

"Hey, look at this one," Kaylee points to one of the smaller sailboats on the dock, *She got the House.* "What does that mean?"

"It means that in their divorce, the wife got the house and he got the boat."

"Oh."

That took the fun out of boat naming.

"Well, no one got the house in our divorce," Kaylee says.

"Yeah. No one got much of anything. Mom's too busy to be happy. Dad lost his family, and you and I got the booby prize: absent parents and no friends."

"We have each other," Kaylee's voice is small and quiet. The question in her voice makes me feel small inside as well.

"Yep, that we do," I say as I give her a shove. "Come on; let's get over to the houseboat section."

I kick my legs into gear and take off. Kaylee squeals behind me, "Wait." The slap of our shoes on the dock sounds like a musical instrument, hollow and deep.

The houseboats are blues, greys, and whites; pinks, lavenders and greens. Some are shingled with no paint. They float along the sides of the docks that run like a maze of streets above the water. They have planks, or bridges that cross from the dock to the deck of each houseboat. Many are lined with beautiful plants, or even small palm trees.

Kaylee and I roam from one dock to another. The homes begin to change the further we get from town.

"Look over there." Kaylee points to a section of houseboats that are smaller and more colorful. "Let's go down there."

There's a gate at the head of the dock. It's been left partly open. I feel like we're trespassing, but I don't say so. The dock creeks as we head down the ramp. The tide is still low, but the smells have settled into my nostrils. I barely notice them.

"These boats are cool."

"Yep. They have a lot of personality." I point to one on the left with brightly painted trims of all different colors. The front door has a painting of a mermaid wearing a beret on her head. On the beret, in small letters, is the word "Dreamcaking." "I wonder what that means."

"Hey, what are you two love birds looking for?"

I look over towards the voice and can't believe what I see. A tall man wearing a purple top hat with a red ribbon coiled around its base like a snake appears out of nowhere. How could we have missed him? He looks like a present wrapped in a rainbow of scarves. One of the scarves is candy cane red and white and it looks as if it was hand knit by a three-year-old. It seems to be unravelling itself around his neck. His purple pants with gold trim look like curtains draped from his waist and down his legs.

"So, did you come to rob a boat? Maybe take a moonlight sail on the bay together?"

Moonlight sail? It's the middle of the day. "She's not my girlfriend." Yuk. No one has ever said that before.

"He's my brother," Kaylee says, as yukked out as I am by the idea. I can tell by the way she announces our status as siblings.

"Ahh. Different mothers or fathers?"

"I'm adopted."

"Adopted, huh. Well, I'm adopted too. I have no parents to speak of. They've been gone since my voice started cracking and my under arms sprouted hair. I am a child of the universe. The sea serpents and mermaids are my parents. They come out at night and sing to me. Have you ever seen them? Scaly green and pink with whiskers as long as your arm. The mermaids are maidens more lovely than any of the legged wenches walking on land."

I try to catch Kaylee's eye but she seems to be hypnotized by him.

"Do you have names you two? Hansel and Gretal? Jack and Jill? I have a name, you know. I've had many names over the years. Which do you want to hear?"

"Which do you want to tell us?" Kaylee doesn't seem afraid.

"Well now, Missy, that's a good question. Who do I want to be today? Man or woman? god or goddess? Saint or Satan?

33

What about you? Who do you want to be today, Sonny boy? Or you, dainty damsel?"

Kaylee looks at me for the first time. I see a smile creeping from the corners of her mouth. "You tell first," she says.

When did Kaylee and Bold start hanging out together?

"Fair enough. I'm Robinson. Robinson Caruso."

Kaylee doesn't miss a beat, "I'm Dr. Doolittle, and this is Dr. Seuss."

He laughs out loud. His mouth open so wide I can see every filling, and quite a few places where he should have teeth but has nothing but gummy space.

"You two are new to these waters, aren't ya?"

"Yes, sir. We just moved here from San Francisco. Our parents separated, and we live with our mom now in Sausalito, but we're going to get to spend time with my dad as soon as he moves into his new place in Mill Valley."

Wow. So much for stranger danger. Kaylee's going to tell this dude our whole life story.

Robinson's mouth stays closed. He puckers his lips as if he'd just sucked on a lemon and nods. "Well, Dr. Doolittle, why don't you and Dr. Seuss come aboard the Good Ship Lollipop," he points at a boat that looks like it might sink any minute. The one window is framed with animals carved from driftwood and painted in stripes, polka dots, and swirls.

"Thanks very much," I tell him as I step sideways and grab Kaylee's arm. I squeeze tightly, "But we have to get going."

"Ow, Flip. That hurts."

"I think Dr. Seuss is giving you a warning, lassy. Am I right, Boss? He's not so sure about Robinson Caruso."

"Well, I'm not worried," Kaylee bursts in before I have a chance to answer. "We've got nowhere to go, and I'd like to see your boat."

"Kaylee," I grab her again. "You can't just go on his boat. We don't even know him."

"Very logical and safe thinking, Boss. But I believe you do know me, remember – I'm Robinson Caruso, also known to my closer friends as Sinbad the Sailor."

I grab Kaylee and pull her close enough that I can whisper in her ear, "This guy's crazy. You can't get on that boat."

Kaylee looks at me and yanks away. "Can we just sit on top of your boat rather than inside of it?"

The guy tugs on one of the scarves around his neck. He closes one eye and tilts his head so far to the side it looks like he might fall over. I don't like the way he looks at me. I think he can read my mind.

Slowly his head comes back to center. "Listen, Boss." Why does he keep calling me that? That's the same name Zorba calls his friend. He's creeping me out. "You look like a sensible lad. You're not sure what to make of me, isn't that so?"

"That's right," I say.

"Life is tricky business. How do we know who to trust and who to avoid? Little Red Riding Hood here has found the strand of golden goodness that runs through my soul. But not you. You seem concerned that I'm going to do you some kind of harm."

I shrug. Why do I feel guilty for mistrusting him? He's crazy. Isn't he? Who dresses like him? Or names themselves after Disney characters?

"I'll tell you what – why don't you and Goldilocks wait right here. I'll go get a few chairs and a table and we'll hold court right here on the dock in plain sight of all my floating neighbors. How's that sound to ya?"

"That sounds fine," Kaylee says before I'm even able to think.

"Well now, Little Big Horn, we need the Boss here to agree before we can sit down and have a pow wow. What do ya say?"

"Why do you keep calling me that? Boss? Zorba calls his friend that. Do you know Zorba?"

"Everyone who's anyone knows Zorba the Greek. He's the king, the captain, the emperor and the high priest of all that holds meaning in life. But how do *you* know Zorba?"

"My father loves him. He gave me his book. I only just started reading it the other day."

"Well now, your father's got good taste in reading materials. That's a hard read for a young deck hand like yourself, but there's a reason he gave it to ya." He cocks his head in the other direction and gives me another one-eyed stare. "I'll tell ya what. Why don't you just call me Zorba."

"I thought we were going to sit together," Kaylee interrupts. I can tell she doesn't like the fact that Zorba's giving me so much attention.

"Well, Boss? What do you say?"

"Fine."

"Well now, that's the spirit," he says as he twirls around in circles then claps his hands together. His laughter doesn't sound human. It's a high pitch that sounds like a train screeching to a halt. Without a word, he skips down the dock to the bridge that boards his boat.

I plop down on the edge of the dock. Kaylee sits beside me. "He's magical, isn't he?"

"Magical? I think he's as crazy as they come. But not totally. He's like a cross between the Cat in the Hat and Willy Wonka."

Kaylee laughs out loud. Her laugh trickles out of her quietly. "I think you're right. Who's this Zorba character you two were talking about?"

"Oh, never mind."

I look around me. The boats on this dock look like they were left out at sea for decades then towed in and donated to an elementary school art project.

I like it here. I like the disorder and the fairy tale feeling of this dock.

"Where'd he go?" Kaylee stands up and heads towards the Good Ship Lollipop.

"Kaylee don't." I stand to stop her, but she's stepped onto Zorba's little dock and is ready to cross the plank to his front door when one of the windows on the side of the houseboat springs open and out pops Zorba like a jack-in-the-box. His scarves dangle from his neck like streamers. His top hat looks like it may fall off his head.

"Ahoy there, maties. You'll have to come back another day. Do come back another day, and we'll sit together and chat.

The winds of today have changed, and I'm going to batten down the hatches and ready myself for the storm."

"What storm?" Kaylee asks, pointing up at the blue sky.

"Well, Rapunzel, storms come from many directions, north and south, inside and out. You carry on with your sunny day while I ready myself for turbulent seas ahead." Zorba closes the window.

"What the heck was he talking about, Flip?"

"I dunno. Let's just go. The guy's a whack job; we should head home."

The window opens again but Zorba's head doesn't pop out. I can hear him well enough though. "Whack job, muddle head, a loon beneath the moon? Maybe so, you'll never know cause your fears will tuck you in like a corpse in a coffin. Your safe little slumber will keep you from knowing. Never knowing. Goodnight Irene, goodnight Irene, I'll catch you in my dreams."

The window closes very slowly. Kaylee starts to cry. "Wait, Mr. Caruso, Zorba. Please don't go. We didn't mean it. I know you're not crazy. I'd like to visit with you."

"Come back another day," he says as he closes the window completely. I hear his last words escape through the crack before the click of the closed window, "The Great Oz has spoken."

"God, Flip, look what you did." Kaylee shoves me aside and stomps up the dock towards the gate. I follow quickly and slam the rickety old gate behind me.

Kaylee's flip flops punish the pavement, slapping it with every step. Then she turns her anger on me. "Why did you have to say those things about him?"

"I don't know. He just seemed crazy to me. Why were you so ready to trust someone who looks like the Mad Hatter? You were ready to get on his boat, Kaylee. That's insane."

Kaylee slows down a bit and her feet ease up on the road. "I know," she says. "But there was something about him that was special. Didn't you feel it?"

I did. I know exactly what she's talking about. He was crazy, in a way. But he was also like a bright light shining itself into the darkness of my heart. It was as if he could see into my soul. He knew me. Knew how afraid I am to take chances now. My own ship is so unsteady these days. It's as if I don't trust myself to step out and begin my life again, here, in this new place where I don't feel I belong. "I did. But still, getting on his boat would have been a really stupid move. Really stupid."

Kaylee nodded just a little bit. Her feet dragged the rest of the way home.

#

I'm an actor in the slow motion film, *The First Day of School*. It's a lousy film, and I wish I wasn't in it.

"Come on kids, we have to be in the car now if we are going to get there on time."

I mutter to myself about not caring if I'm on time. Kaylee says I mutter so much now that I've created a new language called "mutter-nese."

Mom's words pluck Kaylee from her frozen stance in the hallway. She picks up her backpack and heads for the door.

"I'm ready, Mom," she announces, but not in that proud, "see, I'm being a good girl" kind of way. Kaylee walks with slow motion legs too.

"We'll be in the car, Flip. Get your shoes on and get out the door. Now," Mom barks at me.

I want to growl back and bite her.

Why does she have to take us to school anyway? We live about two long city blocks from our new school, Willow Tree Academy. It sounds more like a prison than a school to me. But she insists that she *has* to take us on our first day.

We arrive at school within seconds because that's how long it takes when you drive two city blocks.

The campus is spread out on a hill of green grass. The first building is one story high, not like in the city where our school was three stories – tall and skinny. Willow Tree is like a village with classrooms clumped together in pods scattered along the hillside. Most of the classrooms have a view of the Sausalito Harbor. You can see the boats on the water with their pencil-like masts bouncing up and down.

Kids are moving like ants on the hill. The first bell has already rung and the ants are moving fast. Mom points in the direction of the upper grades – six through eight.

"Your class is up there," she instructs me as if I was some sort of lost kid. We've had the "tour" of the school, and I know where my classroom is.

I'm in seventh grade. I should be in eighth grade, but my parents held me back because of my separation anxiety.

After Kaylee was born, Mom started to go crazy with me hanging from her leg, while Kaylee dangled from her boob. She told my dad he needed to "take over with Felipe" a little more so she could breathe. So, he did, and he and I have been "attached at the hip" ever since. When he used to say that, he'd push his hip into my shoulder because our hips were not at the same level yet, and then we'd try to walk together side by side as if we were attached.

But now we're not attached at the hip. Now we don't even live in the same town.

Mom stands on the hill waiting for me to start up towards class. I wish she'd just get back in her car and go to work.

"Okay, I got it. I can get there on my own. And you don't need to pick us up, either. Kale and I can walk home by ourselves."

Before I turn to walk away, I notice that my Mom's jeans are loose around her waist. They're bunched at the bottom around her shoes. I wonder when she got so skinny that her clothes stopped fitting.

My classroom is much different than the one in the city. There are fewer students, and the chairs and desks are arranged in table groups of four and five. At my old school, they were in straight rows, one right after the other from the front of the room to the back.

I take a seat next to a Latino guy and across from a black girl. There's a small little white guy who looks like he should be in third grade and a desk with no one sitting in it next to him.

The attendance list is like a trip through a dozen different countries. "Diaz, Souza, Goldman, O'Keefe, Al-Zindani, Azam, Bui, Balistreri, and Pereira." I try to match the names with the faces before the owners of both call out "here," but they're too fast.

I hold my math book high in front of my face and peek out the sides. I scan the parts of the room I can see from behind my book. I know I won't find one, but I keep searching for someone I know. It's the worst kind of feeling inside to sit in a room where you don't know one single person.

I hate Willow Tree Academy of Strangers.

Ms. Mason passes out piles of papers. The guy next to me asks, "De donde eres?"

Well that's hardly awkward at all! "I don't understand Spanish," I mumble and look down at the worksheets on my desk.

"Oh, no problem, sorry. Where ya from?"

"San Francisco," I say and then wonder if he means what country I'm from.

"You play ball?"

It doesn't take a rocket scientist to figure out. I have my Giant's cap and coat on today. "Yeah, I was on a team in the city. You play?"

He's leaning back in his chair so far I think he's going to fall backwards. His thick black hair is cut short around his ears, and I notice his eyes are almond-shaped like mine. I bet if I put my arm up against his, our browns would match exactly.

"You bet. I'm Ricki."

He actually sticks his hand out to shake mine. Weird. But I shake it anyways.

"Hey, I'm Flip."

He grins.

"Felipe. Flip for short," I explain.

He nods and then tells me all I need to know to get signed on for the baseball team. We go back to being quiet and wade through the mountain of information on our desks.

At lunch, I hope that Ricki will ask me to sit with him. I would ask him myself but that feels too lame. I watch as he walks off with a bunch of Latino kids. I guess it wouldn't work for me to eat with them anyways. They're all speaking Spanish.

My Spanish abilities begin and end with the following: Hola, me llamo Flip. Tienes un perro? Yo necesito el bano.

A really stimulating seventh grade conversation that in English would be: Hi, my name is Flip. Do you have a dog? I need a bathroom.

I don't think that's going to put me at the top of the popularity list here at Willow Tree Academy of Linguists. I decide to eat my lunch under a tree instead of showing off my language skills.

I think about lunchtime at my old school. Kenny and Jamal are probably talking about the game last weekend. Jamal will give Kenny his bag of chips, and Kenny will pass over his box drink. I wonder if they'll talk about me. I hope they missed me at the game on Saturday.

"Dang, we really needed Simpson at that game. He could've gotten a hit off that pitcher no problem," Kenny would say while he pulled his cap off his head in order to rearrange his hair.

"Yeah, no lie," Jamal would have agreed. "We could have used his 'cheetah feetah' too. We needed those extra runs."

I haven't called Jamal or Kenny since we moved to Sausalito. What's there to say?

"Hey guys. How's it going? Oh, me? Well, I'm fine. My sister and I have become best friends. She and I walk around Sausalito to get ice cream or hang out on the small beach near our house. Sure, it's cool here. Friends? Oh, well, who needs friends really? I've got Kaylee. And my mom, who I never see. And, of course, my dad, who I see even less than my mom."

I stuff my turkey sandwich back into my lunch bag and pull myself up from the ground. I'm done eating. I'm even more done talking to my friends inside my head. That's a pitiful, sorry excuse of a thing to do.

I head back to the classroom. Ms. Mason is sitting behind her desk. She looks up and smiles at me. "Hello there, Felipe. Finished with lunch already?"

"Yes, Ms. Mason. Actually, my name is Flip, not Felipe. No one calls me Felipe."

I hope she's not mad because I corrected her. I don't want to become Felipe here in Sausalito. I'd like to keep my name if that's alright with everyone.

"Oh, sorry. I have it down as Felipe on the roster. I'll be sure to change it, Flip." She opens the roster book to change the mistake. "You can go ahead and have a seat. The bell is going to ring in just a few minutes."

I find my seat, but before I actually sit down, it occurs to me that I'm going to look like a complete and total loser. The other kids will walk in and think that I decided to enjoy my lunch with our teacher today. That is not exactly the impression I'd like to give off on my first day of school.

I turn to leave the room again but the stupid bell goes off. Whatever. I guess I'll start my new career at Willow Tree Academy for Misfits in true style.

When I look up at the clock next, there's only twenty minutes left of class. I want to ask Ricki what he's doing after school but I can't get the words out of my mouth. Not even in English.

The sound of chairs scraping the floor after the bell rings is a different sound than I'm used to. The floors here are tile. The floors in Noe Valley were wood. Metal on tile has a screech to it that can really be annoying.

I'm in no hurry to leave. My classmates run for the door as if the end of the day bell was a fire alarm. I guess they have somewhere to go. I see Kaylee on the hill. She's easy to pick out. She's the stone standing in the rushing river of students.

"Hey Kale." I know she's waiting for me. Who else would she be waiting for? "How'd it go?" I hate to admit it, but it's nice to have someone I know to talk to.

"I guess it was okay. The kids seem pretty nice, and I liked Ms. Avery. I don't like lunch period. How 'bout you?"

"Same here. The only good thing is the baseball season goes all year round, and one of the guys in my class said they need some good hitters."

"Did you tell him you're the home run king?" Kaylee smiles.

"Nah."

Kaylee shrugs. "I guess we're walking home together." She starts down the hill. There's a breeze off the bay and the long white sailboat masts are bobbing like straws in a soda.

"Have you noticed how thin Mom's getting?" Kaylee asks.

"Yeah, tired and thin. I've noticed. Dad too."

Both of our parents are working twice as much to pay for two separate houses. Neither of them seems that much happier now that they're living apart. So I ask you, what's the point? Why ruin a family if you aren't at least going to be *a lot* happier than you were before?

"You want to go back and see Zorba?" Kaylee asks hopefully.

"Nope. But I'll walk to town with you to get some ice cream if you want."

She looks towards the boats in the harbor. You can't see the houseboats from here. "Ok. We'll go visit Zorba another time."

By the time we get home, it's almost 4:30. When I open our new front door, I see Mom on the phone pacing in circles around the front entrance.

"Oh never mind, they've just walked in. I'll speak to you later." She hangs up before whoever was on the other end even has time to say goodbye.

"Where in god's name have you kids been? You told me you were walking home together. School let out at 3:00. Do you know how worried I've been?" She doesn't even take a breath. Her words slap us, one right after the other. Neither of us speaks. We stand completely still and stare at her. This, for some reason, sets her off even more.

"You will never, ever do that again, do you understand?" Slap, slapslapslap. Slap.

"Never do what, Mom? Never go out together for an ice cream cone after school?" My words slap back. *Slap, slapslapslap.*

She looks at the ceiling for a moment. I'm tempted to look there as well but I hold her in my death stare a little longer. Her head inches back to its normal position. She sighs with such force I'm certain the curtains behind us have moved.

"No, I'm glad you went for an ice cream cone. You need to let me know when you aren't coming right home. I worry."

She opens her arms to give one, or both of us, a hug. Kaylee immediately crawls into her loving embrace. I turn away from them and stomp my feet as hard as I can on the wood floors that lead to my room.

"Flip, did you hear what I said?" Mom calls out to me, angry again.

The loud bang of my bedroom door slamming is the only answer she's going to get from me.

CHAPTER FOUR

If I had to rate our first week at Willow Tree Academy of Losers, I'd give it a negative fifty with the possibility of getting better. Maybe.

The "maybe" is only because I have a sliver of hope that I'll be able to "make a friend" out of Ricki. Otherwise, I'd give it a "no hope of crawling out of the hell realm ever" score.

I always thought of myself as an outgoing kind of guy, but the minute I walk into the classroom at Willow Tree Academy of Strangers, it's as if Sure and Sociable were sucked out the soles of my feet. Shy and Silent take their place.

And it's not just because none of the other kids seem to be interested in talking to the new kid in town that the school's scores are in the negative numbers. It's also because I picked up the team practice schedule at school yesterday.

I've read it fourteen times this morning. The words Mondays and Wednesdays swim like sharks in the blurry waters of my eyes. Wednesday – the only weekday I get to be with my father once he moves into his new place.

Our new family structure looks like this: Live with Mom and wave goodbye to her in the morning and say goodnight to her after dinner. Combine that with the new rent-a-dad schedule – every other weekend and Wednesdays – and you have almost no time with either parent. Now some of Dad's rental time will be taken away.

I slump down deeper under the covers and stare at the blank ceiling above me. The sun slices my feet at the end of the bed through a crack in the curtains. An insanely loud crow in the tree outside the house sounds like he's laughing at me. I jump out of bed, rip the curtains to the side, and open the window.

"Get out of here you stupid bird!" I scream and wave my hands in the air. The crow turns its head towards me. His milky grey eyes stare into mine. I slam the window shut and throw myself back onto the bed.

I hate this house. I hate our new school. I hate missing my dad.

I want to hear him whistling in the bathroom. I want to sit with him at breakfast as he reads the baseball stats over pancakes or waffles. I want to hear him say, "Alright-y-o kiddo, I'll see you later," as he walks out the door, knowing that I will.

There's a hole inside of me that only my dad can fill. I stumble and fall into it over and over.

At dinner, I listen for his voice, and then I fall into the hole.

In bed at night, I feel the space where my father used to sit, the weight of his safe, strong body next to mine, and again, I fall into the hole.

The worst part are the conversations I have in my head, the ones I could be having with him, about the game we should be watching together on the television over chips and salsa with an orange juice spritzer. I don't fall into the hole then. The hole sucks me in and swallows me up.

Dad called the other day during a game. "Did you see that play? That guy's body slammed against the ground so hard I thought his head was going to bounce off. And then, when he held his mitt up in the air with the ball in it, well, that was truly something!"

"I know, right?" I say, the blood pumping through my body once again.

The game came alive, full of color and action. The excitement of each play lifted me higher.

"Can you believe he didn't drop it?" My words sail from my mouth, no longer blocked by the dry tightness in my throat.

We watched play by play, together through two innings. Then he had to go. I hung up the phone and everything around me turned to black and white again.

When I think of that phone call now, it seems like the fifth-place ribbon in a race I've spent my entire life training for.

I crumple the schedule in my fist and throw it onto the floor. I pull my t-shirt from the drawer: Mondays and Wednesdays. I yank my pants out from under the chair. They won't let go. I yank harder and the chair falls over: Mondays and Wednesdays. I take note of the room before closing the door. The walls and shelves are empty. My baseball heroes wait in boxes stacked in the corner of my room. I need those memories to stay safe in one small space.

Mom and Kaylee are in the kitchen. Kaylee sits at the table and talks to Mom's backside while she does their breakfast dishes.

"Hey, Flip, you're almost in time for lunch, lazy bones." Kaylee smiles until she sees my face.

I have to fight hard not to scream at her. I clamp my lips shut, wrapping them around my teeth. My breath blows through my nostrils like gusts of hot summer wind.

"Good morning, Flip," Mom says without turning around and gathering the information she should have before greeting me in her chipper, sing-songy voice. "I was just telling your sister that I've been able to pick up some extra hours at the massage clinic. I'll be working later during the week. I know it's not ideal. It means you'll have to come home to an empty house."

She doesn't see it coming. My words are a sucker punch to the soft part of her belly. "We already come back to an empty house, Mom. Every day. We're half a family in a house that isn't a home. What difference will it make if you're here late?"

Kaylee gasps. "Flip."

Mom wipes her hands on the dishtowel and turns slowly from the sink. She looks first at Kaylee, then at me. "I know you're angry, Flip. If your father and I could've done it differently we would've. We were hurting each other too much. We needed that to stop."

Her weight shifts from her right foot to her left. She puts the dishtowel on the counter behind her, then picks it up again. "I'm sorry." She looks straight at me.

"I got my practice schedule." I don't want to hear how she and Dad would have done it differently if they could. "I have practice on Wednesdays. *Wednesdays*! That means that the one lousy day a week I get to see my dad is going to be taken up by baseball. Now I have to make a choice between the two things I love the most, and that's your fault!" I jump out of my chair and fling it out of my way. It slams down on its side.

Mom tries to grab me with promises she can't keep. "Flip, we'll figure something out. I'll talk to your father."

Kaylee surprises me. She jumps up from her chair and moves towards me. Her words hit Mom low and hard, "There's nothing to figure out. Can't you see? Nothing can make this better. We want our old life back."

Mom's shoulders sag; her head drops. She turns back to the sink and mutters, "I can't bring our old life back. We'll have to figure out a way to live with the one we have."

I walk out of the kitchen with Kaylee by my side. We sit on the front stoop. Kaylee listens to the air around me and waits. My head falls between my knees and I squeeze.

Kaylee whispers, but I don't catch her words.

"*What*?" I know I shouldn't snap at her.

"I said, do you want to walk to Schoonmacher beach with me?"

Her braid hangs over her shoulder. It reminds me of a bell pull. I have a strong urge to yank on it to see if her head will ring. Instead, I weigh my options. I don't have many. I can either spend the day avoiding Mom and rereading the practice schedule, or get the heck away from this stupid house.

"Ok. Sure. Let's go kayaking. We have to get our allowance from Mom. You do it."

"Me? How can we go ask Mom for money after what just happened?"

"I dunno," I say, but I get up and walk inside. Kaylee follows behind me.

Mom is sitting at the kitchen table, a glass of water half empty in front of her. "We're going to Schoonmacher. Can we have our allowance?" The coldness of my words causes an ache in my chest.

"Get my wallet," she says without looking up at either of us. "It's in my purse on the table in the hall."

In that moment, I want to fix what feels broken between us but I don't have the words. I know it can't be all Mom's fault that she and Dad split up. I'm sure there's something about Dad that made Mom so unhappy. Why was he such a disappointment to her? Well, what I know is that he's my rock. I need him to be my rock.

I grab her purse and place it on the kitchen table.

Kaylee says nothing. I can see how she wants to run to our mother. But she doesn't. She stands behind me.

Mom's fingers slip into the folds of her wallet. Out comes a ten-dollar bill. "This is for both of you for the week." She hands me the bill and drops the wallet back into her purse. "You kids know the rules. You stay in the lagoon area at all times."

"I *know* the rules, Mom."

My words bite harder than I'd intended. I'm sorry the minute they come out of my mouth.

"We'll be careful," Kaylee says quietly. "We've been going there for weeks now. Kids don't leave the lagoon area." The room softens around the edges of her voice.

"Ok. I'll see you later." Mom picks up her glass of water, finishing what's left in one long gulp.

Kaylee and I had discovered Schoonmacher Beach one day after school. Kids from Willow Tree Academy of the Playful were in the water, climbing over and swimming under red, blue, and yellow plastic kayaks. One of the kayak rental owners, Harley, offered us a free kayak to play on.

"Let's go out to the houseboats today," I announce as we leave our little neighborhood of small white houses and head for the water.

"Seriously? You want to paddle out into the Bay? We're not allowed to do that. Mom told us before we left not to leave the lagoon. What if the current takes us away?"

I roll my eyes.

"Come on, Kale, where could it possibly take us? We're miles from the Golden Gate Bridge. Even if we drifted, we'd just end up in Strawberry, or Tiburon. What's the big deal?"

Kaylee looks towards the beach; families have their blankets spread out along the water's edge. Children of all ages are digging holes and filling bright colored buckets with sand. Moms and dads are sprawled on towels beside one another; happy little families posing for the perfect photo.

"Fine, whatever," Kaylee snaps. "You better hope Mom doesn't find out."

I shrug my shoulders. "I don't really care if she does."

Harley isn't working. A dark haired surfer dude named Nate is. He doesn't even look at the form when I hand it in. Harley never asks us to fill out the forms that ask for our names, time of departure, and kayaking experience.

The truth is, Kale and I have hardly any experience. I put down that we have plenty and check off "yes" where it asks if we've been given the training. I don't know why they ask since at the bottom of the page it says in bold print: Children under 16 must be accompanied by experienced kayakers outside the lagoon.

Nate doesn't know Harley gives us the kayak for free so we hand him ten bucks and that's that. We're good to go.

"Ok, kids, see you back here in an hour."

Nate drags our bright yellow kayak down to the waterfront. It's a blue sky day out over the bay. The fog behind us grabs the top of the hills in its massive white hand. It curls its fingers into a fist that promises to pound the blue out of the sky sometime soon.

Life vests on, we jump into the kayak and start paddling, first inside the small area of the Schoonmacher cove, and then through the gateway out into the Bay.

"Flip, what if they see us leaving? He's going to notice two kids leaving the lagoon. We're going to get in so much trouble for this."

"Let's go towards the houseboats." I ignore the worried chatter that blows around me in my seat behind her. It feels good to be on the water, away from the house in Sausalito.

A splash of cold, salty wet hits my face. Kaylee's paddle slaps the surface of the water, spraying me like a sprinkler.

"Hey, Kale – keep it in the water. You're getting me wet."

"I'm trying," she whines. "It's harder out here; the current is strong."

She digs the blade of the paddle in carefully, pulling back as the boat glides forward.

"Kale, look." A heap of seals or sea lions – I never know the difference – covers every inch of the dock. "Look at their eyes."

We both stop paddling and glide beside the blubbery blobs of brown on the dock. A seal pops up beside our boat. Kaylee screams. It disappears under the water again.

"Oh my god, Flip, what if he pops up under our boat?"

"Well, I guess we'll get wet," I smile, but I'm a little nervous about that, too.

We reach the maze of houseboats. Funky, falling-apart houses with shutters that dangle and shingles that are broken and worn float beside homes that look like castles and doll houses.

We drift on for a time while the fog's fist opens out over the water. It stirs the wind around us.

Kenny and Tyson would love it out here. I bet if we each had our own boats, we'd be racing back to the lagoon. I imagine Kenny screaming as Tyson pulls up behind him and tosses a paddle of water into his face. I miss my friends. I feel a rush of red hot mad rise behind my eyes. It bleeds down into my cheeks. Why did they have to split up? Why couldn't my parents have worked harder to stay together?

"Why do you think they split up?" I'm surprised by the words that dart out of my mouth before I have a chance to stop them with my teeth.

"What?" Kaylee looks back at me, as if she'd forgotten I was there. "What are you talking about?"

"What do you think I'm talking about? How many other people do you know who have split up lately?"

Kaylee's body rocks with the movement of the boat. Just when I think she's going to pretend I never asked, she answers. "I don't know, Flip." Her face is screwed up into a knot, and I see the tears waiting to run down her cheeks. "Sometimes I wonder if it was us. If maybe we argued too much, or took too much of their love time with all our activities and stuff. But then I think – lots of kids are busier than us, and their parents aren't split up."

I'm relieved to hear that I'm not the only one who thinks it might be our fault. I've been thinking about it a lot. I have long arguments with myself in my head: *It probably has something to do with you. Mom probably feels how much more connected you are with Dad. They probably fight about it. Maybe Mom thinks if she kicks Dad out of the house she and you will get closer.*

No, fool. That's ridiculous. Mom knows you love her. Boys always like their Dads more. And anyway, Mom is the one that filled her heart with her love for Kaylee. From the day she was born it was obvious that Mom loved Kaylee differently than she did you.

A gust of wind so strong slaps us and rocks the boat. Kaylee chirps like a bird and grabs the side of the boat. "Oh my god. Where did that wind come from?"

"Let's head out," I say to the back of Kaylee's head. "Before it gets worse."

We turn the boat around and plunge our paddles into the water's choppy thick surface. The water holds us in place. Or is it the wind?

"Come on, Kaylee, paddle harder. We're not moving."

We paddle harder. It's as if someone has tied a rope to our kayak and is pulling us backwards. We're working so hard and getting almost nowhere. I can tell Kaylee's arms are getting tired. Her paddle begins to slap the water.

"Kaylee! Keep it in the water."

"Flip, I'm trying. We're going sideways. Steer the boat. That's your job." The kayak is sliding across the water, the wind and currents pushing it sideways.

"Watch out!" Kaylee shrieks as the side of the kayak smashes into a sailboat. Where did that come from? Kaylee's paddle gets caught between the two boats along with her hand. She screams out in pain and drops the paddle. It slides down into the dark waters.

"Oh no, Kale, get it. Quick. You have to get the paddle."

Kaylee is crying.

"Get it, Kaylee," I shout at her. She's sobbing now but makes a lame attempt to push off the sailboat to get the paddle. The wind shoves us back into the boat. Kaylee screams. Her hand is caught between the two boats again.

"Oh man, we are so screwed." I stand up and lean over the side, reaching towards the water. The kayak rocks. Kaylee screams.

"Flip, sit down!"

I do.

"We have to get away from this sailboat."

"No. We can't. If we do, we'll get blown across the bay. It's the only thing keeping us from being carried all the way to San Francisco."

Another strong blast of wind pushes us further from the boat. Our paddle floats free.

"We have to get it!" My scream blows back into my face.

"Oh god, Flip, what are we going to do? This is not fun at all."

Something about the way Kaylee says this cracks me up. "Really? You're not having fun yet?" I begin to laugh. I know it's not funny, but there are nervous fingers tickling my insides. I laugh harder.

"Why the heck are you laughing? You're crazy, Flip. This was such a bad idea. *Your idea!* Mom is going to kill us, if we ever make it back home again!"

I glare at her. The nervous fingers turn to a fist that punches me in the gut. I imagine our mother when we tell her what we've done.

"She won't find out if no one tells her," I threaten Kaylee.

"I'm not going to tell, Flip, but..."

"Hey kids." Nate, the dark-haired surfer dude, pulls up beside us in a small motorized dinghy. "Hold out your paddle." He cuts the motor and lets the boat glide closer.

"Oh my god, are we glad to see you." Kaylee sounds so desperate it makes me cringe.

"The wind picked up out of nowhere. You guys weren't supposed to leave the lagoon, I thought you knew that." Nate expertly pulls us in towards his boat. Holding the end of my paddle, he ties a rope to the front of our kayak.

"We lost the other paddle." Kaylee points to the lone paddle making its way along the surface of the choppy waters.

Nate brings our boat and his over to the paddle, scoops it up and heads back with us to the cove. The wind and the motor drown out the sound of my warning to Kaylee. "Don't rat me out, Kaylee. Don't tell anyone I lied on the forms, okay?"

Kaylee stares at me. In that moment, I think she hates me. I don't blame her. I forced her to come out here and almost got us killed. The urge I have to rip my hair out of my head in handfuls persists.

"I will never leave this little cove again." Kaylee glares at me.

Nate swings the boat around and lets go of the line attached to our kayak. "Alright kids, you can bring her in the rest of the way. I'm going back out to rescue other stranded sailors."

"Thank you *so* much," Kaylee gushes. She might as well be on the ground kissing his feet it's so over the top.

"Yeah – thanks," I say.

"No worries, guys. Just pull her up to the shore." He turns the dinghy towards the open bay once more. "And for the future – you're not allowed to take the boats outside the lagoon."

"Okay. Sorry." Kaylee's teeth are clenched. I expect to hear her growl.

My teeth chatter and my whole body shakes furiously. I'm freezing.

"Flip, you're sopping wet."

"Yeah, I wonder how I got that way? Sitting behind you in a kayak is like being hosed down by a fire fighter."

Kaylee begins to giggle, and then the two of us let go.

"I'm surprised we didn't sink, we took on so much water. Your paddle was like a giant soup spoon the way you were dumping water into the boat," I tease her. It feels good.

We laugh on the way home. The closer we get to the house, the less happy we feel.

"Seriously, Kale, you can't tell Mom about leaving the lagoon. She'll never let us kayak again."

"Oh bummer! Like I really want to do that again!"

"If she finds out, we'll be grounded forever," I plead.

"So? It's not like we have anywhere to go, or anyone to see." Kaylee's words are so bitter they burn.

"We just don't. We – just – don't – tell. We can't, Kaylee. We broke so many rules today. I lied on the form; we totally disobeyed Mom."

Kaylee looks like she's going to cry.

"I really need to count on you, Kale. Please. I'll be in so much trouble, please!"

"Okay," she says.

I'm afraid. There's nothing I can do but wait and see.

Kaylee stops in front of the house. She looks down at her hand. Shock spreads across her face. "How am I going to explain *this*?"

She throws her bruised hand in my face. A wide purplish blue stripe runs across the base of her knuckles.

"Just don't let her see it, I guess." I act cool but inside I feel sick with how badly she smashed her hand.

"Oh great, that's going to be really easy," she hisses.

"You can make something up, Kale, it's not that hard. Tell her the truth – your hand got smashed between the kayak and another boat – just don't say where we were when it happened."

Kaylee nods and follows me into the house. As soon as the front door closes behind us, Mom calls out from upstairs.

"Kaylee, Flip, is that you?"

"No, Mom, it's someone else," I mutter. The mad is stuck to my tongue when I speak to Mom. No matter what I say, it just comes out nasty.

Kaylee smirks and then quickly answers, "Yeah, Mom, it's us."

Mom stands at the top of the stairs looking down on us like the Wizard of Oz. "Did you have fun?" Not very wizardly. There's a longing in her voice that annoys me.

"Yeah, it was fine. We're wet. We need to change."

I wait for Kaylee. She stands at the bottom of the stairs. She looks down at her hand and then up at Mom. My heart stops. I listen for what I don't want to hear.

"We had fun," she says and pulls herself away from the staircase. "I need to change."

We walk down the hall together. I nod to her and then close my door behind me.

#

The quiet in our kitchen is like a thin sheet of ice waiting to be cracked. "Pass the salt, Kale." My voice is the rock that shatters the ice. Kaylee reaches for the salt shaker in front of her plate.

"Kaylee, what did you do to your hand?" Mom takes Kaylee's hand in her own. Kaylee pulls it away quickly and puts it in her lap. She looks up at me. "Be cool," I tell her with my eyes. I look down at my plate and hold my breath.

"Kaylee? How did you bruise your hand?"

"It's fine, Mom. It got smashed between a boat when we were kayaking." Kaylee doesn't look her in the eye. She spins her spaghetti round and round on the fork until there is such a huge bundle she has to drop it all off and start again.

"How did you hit another boat? The lagoon doesn't have boats moored inside its docks. You kids didn't leave the lagoon, did you?"

"No!" This is new territory for both of us. I don't trust my sister. "There were other kids there too, Mom. We were having splash wars and Kaylee's hand got caught between another kayak and ours, that's all."

Kaylee continues to study her spaghetti as it spins on her fork.

"What's going on you two? Are you telling me the truth? Kaylee, look at me."

The sharp hook of Mom's tone annoys Kaylee. Her words come out strong and sure. "Mom, I got my hand caught between the kayaks. It's no big deal." She holds Mom's stare. For a long time. She lowers the blaze of her gaze, but not before she's singed Mom's eyebrows.

Mom sighs. "I need to be able to trust you two. I am happy that you're able to wander freely in Sausalito, and that you've found a place to be with other kids, but I need to know that you're making good choices and staying safe."

"We are, Mom. We just went to the lagoon. What's the big deal?" I snap.

Mom's expression softens as she looks over at my sister. "Kale, honey, let's put some Arnica on those bruises after dinner."

Kaylee looks like she wants to cry. "Okay, Mom."

The regret of our lies settles in like an unwanted neighbor stopping by for a visit.

#

"I'm going to the houseboats after school today."

"Okay, I'll go with you." I've been thinking about Zorba of the houseboats a lot. I keep trying to read the book Dad gave me but it drags like a math class before lunch. I'm only able to read bits and pieces, mostly the conversations he has with his friend.

"Really?" Kaylee sounds like someone just offered her a trip to the amusement park.

"Yeah, why not? I don't know if he'll even want to talk to us, but I'm willing to try. We can't go on board his boat, okay? I still think he's a nut job, and I don't want to be held hostage on the Good Ship Lollipop with a man who thinks he's Sinbad the Sailor."

"Or Zorba the Greek," Kaylee adds, flashing a smile my way. I wonder if she would've gone to see him without me.

It's high tide. The salty seaweed smell is gone. The breeze has taken all the smells out across the water. A grey and white seagull circles overhead, his high-pitched screech calls out like an alarm. Just as we reach the gate to Zorba's dock, a tall woman with long blonde hair, high black boots, and a small white poodle in her arms stops in front of the gate on her way out. I notice she has long purple streaks running through her hair and one long green feather woven beside it.

"Hi there, kids. Are you here to visit someone in particular?"

"Ahh, well, yes. We came to see, um," Kaylee looks to me for help.

"We're here to visit with the guy on the Good Ship Lollipop."

"Robin? You're here to see Robin? Well, I just saw him a little while ago. He's having a good day today, so you're lucky. How do you know Robin?" Her accent sounds like one of my mother's sisters from New York City, twangy and sharp.

"We're just friends."

"Huh. Alright then. Me and Stella gotta go get some groceries." She pushes past Kaylee and me. We step through the gate and down the ramp to the dock leading to Zorba's boat.

"What do you think she meant when she said he's having a good day?" Kaylee asks.

"I don't know, but I'm betting that first day we saw him wasn't one of his better days."

There's no sign of Zorba around his boat or on the docks. His window and door are both wide open.

"What are we supposed to call him? Sinbad? Robin? Robinson?"

"I'm sticking with Zorba," I tell her. "It fits."

Zorba must have heard us talking because he pops his head out the window and then in again like a Cuckoo Clock.

When he steps out onto the deck, I'm shocked. He looks so different. He's taken off all the scarves but the red and white striped one. The top hat is gone but he's still wearing his tie dye shirt and jacket. He's no longer wearing the purple curtains with the gold trim; he's got on normal jeans now.

"Well, well, look who's here. Dr. Seuss and Dr. Doolittle."

Kaylee smiles. "You remembered."

"Of course I did. How could I forget? What brings you back to the Good Ship? Ready for that cup of tea and cookies now, Boss?"

I'm glad he's still calling me Boss. "Yep, I'm ready."

"Well then, come aboard, maties. We'll sit on the front deck here in plain view of the whole world. Come along, that's it. Watch your step, Cinderella – we don't want any glass slippers falling into the muddy waters below."

Even though he still sounds a bit crazy, his eyes aren't darting about like a ping pong ball. He holds my gaze in a normal way and smiles. "Come aboard, Boss. Glad to see you've decided to crawl out of the coffin and into the world of make-believe."

It occurs to me my parents would kill me if they knew we were here. I step aboard the Good Ship and follow Zorba and my sister to the front deck of the boat.

He points to a circle of tree stumps and says, "Sit." Then he disappears into his house. I wonder if he'll come out again.

He does. He has a bag of chips and a few sodas. He sits across from us in the circle of stumps. "So, my little land lubbers, what brings you back to the Good Ship Lollipop? Don't you have better things to do than to hang out with a nut job like me?" He smiles when he says this. I notice how blue his eyes are. I swear they were a different color the other day. Is that possible?

"We just wanted to talk." Kaylee is nervous. Her voice wobbles. "We like you."

Zorba's head tilts backwards and he opens his mouth wide to laugh. He doesn't say anything, though. He just laughs. Maybe this isn't one of his "good days" after all.

"Did your parents really die when you were young?" I ask the question that has been burning inside of me since we met him last. I want to know if he really is an orphan.

He looks at me with such intensity I wish I could take it back.

"You don't have to talk about it if you don't want." Kaylee comes to the rescue.

"That's a big question for such a small day. But I'll answer it. Only my mother died. I'm told that my father sailed into town and dropped anchor only long enough to leave me behind in the womb of my mother's ship. She gave birth to me here, on the Good Ship, with the help of her community. Those were wild times, the sixties. There was a kind of freedom that was carefree and careless. My mother loved both. When I was about your age, Thumbelina, my mother's ship sailed off into the sunset without me. She danced with Careless a bit too long, and the sting of Satan entered her veins and took her from me."

Zorba's eyes close. I look over at Kaylee. I can tell she doesn't understand what he's talking about. I do though, and I feel bad for asking.

"Who raised you then?" Kaylee turns the conversation away from sad.

"I told you before," he snaps. "I am a child of the universe, raised by mermaids and sea serpents."

I don't know what to believe. I wonder if any of what comes out of this guy's mouth is true, or if it's all just a part of his fairytale life.

Kaylee's eyes begin to fill with tears. I think he scared her. I'm about to tell her we should leave when he starts to talk again.

"You want the true story, don't you, Snow White?" He reminds me of Jerry, the way he gives Kaylee a new name every time he talks to her. How does he do that? He reaches inside of our lives and pulls out these pieces of information he can't possibly know.

"It was the wonder of those times. Community was everything here on the docks. I had uncles, and aunts, grandmas and grandpas to look after me. None of them were blood relatives, but they were my family. They were my mermaids and sea serpents. You see?"

Kaylee nods her head and gives him a half smile. He turns to look at me. "What about you, Boss? How did you end up an orphan? How did your tug boat land you so far from your mother ship?"

"I don't know. I have no idea why my first mother didn't keep me. I don't know where she lives, what she looks like. Nothing. All I know is my parents wanted a child, and they brought me here from Guatemala to be their kid."

Kaylee's eyes open wide for a split second. Then she whispers, "I'm glad they did."

Zorba smiles that big smile again. "Isn't the world a marvelous place? The seas of life bring us together, like two boats on the water's windy surface colliding. Tell me something I need to know, Mary Poppins." Zorba looks at Kaylee.

"Our parents split up. We don't know why. I think it might be our fault. Flip does too."

"Kaylee, are you crazy?" I look at Zorba. A smile leaks across his face slowly.

"Well now, my little truth teller, what makes you think that?"

"Because why else would they stop loving each other? If they were happy before we came, happy enough to get married, what else could have gotten in the way of that love?"

Zorba tips his head and closes one eye, the same way he did the other day. "Is that true, Boss? Is that how you see it, too?"

"I don't want to talk about this. Kaylee, why are you telling him this stuff?"

"Because if I don't tell someone I'm going to explode. And anyways, we can trust him. Right? Can't we?" Kaylee's eyes lock with Zorba's like the jaws of a dog around a bone. She won't let go. He holds her gaze until she does.

"That's right, Lady Chatter-chops. The Good Ship holds all the secrets of the seas."

"See?" Kaylee looks at me with such confidence I want to punch her. "I told you."

"Kaylee, you're an idiot," I say and stand to leave. "I'm going home. You need to come with me."

"Now hold on a minute there. I want to show you something." Zorba jumps straight up into the air as if he were on a pogo stick. He launches himself forward and into the boat.

He comes out with a plastic grocery bag stuffed full of something. When he sits back down again, I see balls and clumps of different colored yarns stuffed tightly into the bag. I flash a question-mark look at Kaylee, who smiles and shrugs.

Zorba pulls the candy cane scarf from his neck. "Ok. Look at this scarf. Two different colored yarns knit beautifully together to make a warm blanket of love."

Kaylee isn't able to hold back her giggles. I begin to laugh as well. Zorba's beautifully knit scarf has huge holes all over it where the strands of yarn have pulled apart.

I watch to see if Zorba realizes we are laughing at his scarf. If he does, he doesn't seem to mind because now he's laughing with us.

"Did you make that scarf?" Kaylee asks.

"Yes, my little Drummer Girl, yes I did. One of my mothers taught me how to knit when I was young. She thought it would help with my anxieties and such."

"Did it?" I ask.

"Perhaps. Perhaps. It may have. But then again, it may not have, too."

Jeesh, this guy can't ever just answer a question directly.

"A strand of red and a strand of white are woven together in beauty and happiness. Do you see my meaning?"

"No," Kaylee says.

"Yes. I see it. A mother and a father."

"Right, Boss, or a man and a woman, or two women, two men, it doesn't matter. Two people come together and weave a life. Their bond is secure and tight. But just like this scarf, life pulls and tugs on the strands of connection and they begin to loosen. If they were knit really tightly, it may take more tugging but eventually, life will pull on this scarf."

Zorba reaches into the plastic bag and pulls out a blue and a green piece of yarn and a crochet hook.

"My mom used to crochet hats," Kaylee says.

Zorba doesn't speak. He takes a piece of blue yarn and pulls it through from one end of the scarf to the other, weaving it between the red and white. Then he does the same with the green.

"Alright then. I've just added two strands to the scarf. Now I ask you, did those two strands weaken or strengthen this scarf?"

"They made it stronger." Kaylee hops off her stump. "That's us. We are the blue and green. And you are saying that adding us to the scarf, to our parents' lives, didn't make their bond weaker, it made it stronger."

"That's right, my little starfish. Adding yarn doesn't weaken the weave. But look what happens if I keep tugging at the scarf down here, say, in the parts that were woven before you came along that were already a bit loose and wobbly. Even though the blue and green don't make the scarf weaker, they can't hold the whole thing together. Life may just come in and pull those strands apart despite the fact that the scarf is made more beautiful and interesting with the new colors."

Something inside of me says Zorba's explanation for our family is too simple. Foolish even. But I want to believe he's right. Kaylee and I didn't pull our parents apart. The fabric of their relationship must have already been loose. Zorba's eyes are smiling and he's beaming them at me. I feel a rainbow of warmth and color skittering across my body. It makes me want to laugh. Zorba sees it and he starts to laugh. Kaylee joins in, and soon I, too, am laughing aloud. Over what, I do not know, but the laughter feels so good, and it's reaching down so deep inside of me that I never want it to end.

"I like your visits. I like your secrets. Don't worry, Boss, I won't tell a soul. We all feel tangled and confused inside from time to time. You'll find the place in the knot that loosens. Just tug lightly and it will give soon enough. You'll see." He puts a hand on my shoulder. "Remember, Boss, life's a tricky business. You've got to trust someone along the way until you trust yourself just enough to go it alone."

Zorba pretends to tip his hat and bows to Kaylee. "And you, my little blossom of youth, you stick with the Boss. He needs you on board for now." Zorba stands and moves towards the dock. "Come along now, I've work to do. I hope you visit again soon, though. I think we have much to learn from one another. Don't you?"

Kaylee stands slowly. I can see she doesn't want to leave. Neither do I.

"Yes, I think we do," she says and moves towards Zorba. "I think we will be good friends, Zorba."

Zorba's laughter sails across the front of the boat and around the docks. It carries us away like two kites on a full breeze.

CHAPTER FIVE

Kaylee walks beside me on our way home from another thrilling day of school. My sister is by my side so much of the time I might as well start wearing overalls. We could call ourselves Thing One and Thing Two.

It's getting a bit better here, north of the Golden Gate Bridge, in the Magical County of Marin. Although I haven't mastered the art of making friends at Willow Tree Academy of the Unfriendly, we still have Zorba, and, most days, Kaylee and I find a way to keep ourselves entertained.

I do miss having friends of my own, though. I don't know why none of the kids seem interested in me. I never realized how your friends are the frame that holds the picture of who you are. I don't know who I am here.

I thought maybe once the guys on the Willow Tree Academy's Need a Personality baseball team got to know me, I'd start to make some friends and have a place to go after school. It hasn't happened yet.

The other day I tried to talk with Damion, one of the guys on the team. He's a decent hitter, and the two of us can get around the bases most times we're up. I tried talking to him after practice the other day. I swear the expression on his face made me want to check the bottom of my shoes for dog crap. I don't get it. When I make a killer catch, or slam one into the outfield, my teammates don't whack me on the back as I slap home plate with my cleats. They sit in the dugout and roll their eyes. I haven't heard it, but I imagine they nudge one another and whisper, "There he goes again. The cocky kid from SF trying to make us all look bad."

Kaylee and I cut across the little square of green we call a yard to the white shingled house that we now call home. Kaylee gets the key out from under a stone in the backyard first and pushes the door open. "Hello?"

Does she expect someone to respond? Mom has taken more shifts at the Massage Clinic. She doesn't get home until after seven some days.

Kaylee looks around the kitchen as if she's waiting for Mom to pop out of the pantry with a plate of cookies and milk.

"Really, Kale? Which part of, 'I won't be home until seven,' did you not understand?"

Kaylee shrugs and drops her backpack on the chair. She glances at the note Mom left on the table for us. It's called, "parenting by paper." You know, guiding your kids into adulthood through instructional notes left on the kitchen table, along with endless bowls of pasta in the fridge.

"I dunno," Kaylee says. "You never know, maybe she had a cancellation or something."

"Mmm, maybe. And maybe she won the lottery and didn't even go to work today!"

Kaylee goes to the fridge. I can tell I hurt her feelings again. I think she might climb in and sit among the cartons of milk and juice and close the door behind her. I reach in around her and grab the orange juice and leave her to stare at the mayonnaise jar.

On my way to the TV room, I read the note Mom left on the table. "Hi kids. There's leftover pasta in the fridge for dinner. I'll be home by seven. Please do your homework and your dishes. Love Mom."

I guzzle a ton of OJ right out of the carton. Why not? It's not like anyone is going to tell me not to, right?

I turn the television on and take my place on the couch. I think about Zorba. I want to know what it is about Zorba the Greek that my father loves so much. Our Zorba pops into my head at the same time the phone rings.

"I got it," I tell Kaylee and leap over the side of the couch.

"Hello?"

"Hey Flip, it's Dad."

"Oh, hey Dad, I was just thinking about you. Well actually, I was thinking about Zorba the Greek."

"Oh, you started the book? What do you think of old Zorba?" I want to tell him about our Zorba. Will he flip out and tell us not to go visit some crazy man on a boat?

"I only just met him. It's a hard book to follow. The Book Worm is kind of a sad fellow. I'm glad he and Zorba meet."

"Yes. Zorba helps him realize the ways he's let life pass him by. Zorba's love for life is infectious, isn't it? The Book Worm has no choice but to live life more fully when he's with Zorba."

"Exactly. He has no fear. He just lives his life out loud and doesn't care what anyone thinks."

"Sounds like you're really enjoying the book, son. I know it's not exactly a kid's book, but stick with it if you can. It's a wonderful read." Dad's voice is like warm cookies and milk.

"What's up, Dad? How come you called?"

"Well, I'm calling with some bad news, I'm afraid."

The milk sours and the cookies crumble. I already know what he's going to say. "You can't see us this weekend, right?"

"Actually, yes. That's right. I'm really sorry. The job up north has turned into a nightmare and I'm going to have to spend Saturday there."

"But we can see you on Sunday?" Please, please, please say yes.

"I just don't know, son. I don't want to make any promises. I'll have to let you know Saturday night when I get home."

"Why can't you just pick us up Saturday after work if you don't have to work Sunday? At least we can have one night together. Please, Dad? I really miss you."

My pleading sounds like it did when I was little, begging for ice cream or one more ride on his shoulders.

"Okay Flip, if I don't have to go back on Sunday I'll pick you up after work. I'll call you in the afternoon. I'm sure I'll know by then what's happening."

There's a long silence on the line. I have nothing left to say and it looks like he doesn't either. "Okay Flip, I'll talk to you Saturday. Love you."

"Love you too." I hang up. I stare at the muted television. The actors carry on with their conversations. Smiles, laughter and close-up shots of perfect teeth and pretty faces are plastered across the screen. I throw the clicker onto the floor and walk into the kitchen.

"Screw this," I say loudly. My sister looks up from her math homework. "I'm tired of sitting in front of the TV."

"There's leftover pasta in the fridge for dinner." She winces when she says it. Even Kaylee knows that leftover pasta in the fridge is not worth mentioning.

"You know what? I'm sick of leftover pasta, too. Let's go downtown and get a burger. You want to?"

Kaylee looks down at Mom's note as if it's going to say something specific about not going out for burgers after a certain time, or maybe that she would prefer we stay home until she gets there – but it doesn't. Her neatly printed letters assume that her children will be home, safe and sound, doing their homework and washing their dishes.

"I guess," Kaylee says, although I can tell by the tone of her voice she's not as sick of pasta and staying home as I am.

"Great, let's go. We have to beat Mom home, and it's already four."

"Are we going all the way downtown?" Oh no, here it comes, the Worrier.

"Yeah, where'd you think we were going to get burgers – the movie theater?"

I pull my wallet out of my back pocket and check to see if I have any cash. Having no social life is good for saving money. I grab the house key off the kitchen table to place back under the stone and stand there to see if Kaylee is going to follow.

Yep. She leaves her books sitting open on the kitchen table and heads out the door behind me.

The hamburger joint is filled with older kids from the eighth grade track team. They're dressed in their bright blue silky running shorts and team shirts. I feel like a loser here with my little sister. We grab our food and take it to a table in the far back corner.

I'm concentrating so hard on my fries that I don't realize the voice above me is talking to me.

"Earth to Flip," Kaylee says. I look up at her and see Ricki standing beside our table.

"Oh hey, where'd you come from?"

"My mother's womb, I suppose." Ricki cracks up at his own joke. Kaylee laughs too hard and too long. I wish I was here alone.

"Can I sit with you?" Ricki pulls the chair out before I answer and plops a big basket of fries on the table.

"Wow, that's a healthy dinner." I watch to see if he gets that I'm joking.

"Dinner? You kidding? This is a mid-late afternoon on-the-way-home-for-dinner snack. This plate of fries won't fill my left cavity."

"Wow, you must have a mega big cavity in your tooth," Kaylee smirks. Ricki is nice and laughs.

The silence feels awkward. I shovel fries into my mouth faster than I can chew and swallow. I stop. Ricki pours hot sauce on his fries as if it was ketchup.

"Holy, holy that's gotta burn," I say.

"Nope, not for me. My mother put hot sauce in my baby bottle and all over my pacifier. Pretty sure my taste buds were hot sauce radiated right off my tongue before I could talk." He pops several fries in at once. Kaylee and I watch carefully for a reaction. "Maybe that's why we Latinos speak Spanish so fast. By the time we were learning to talk, our tongues were racing to get out of our mouths and our words were hoping to follow."

Now I laugh loud and long. I like Ricki. I hope I don't blow it and say something stupid. I'd really like to have him for a friend.

"So, are you going to introduce me to your date here?" Ricki points to Kaylee with a fry so soaked in hot sauce it's soggy.

"Oh. Yeah, sorry. This is my sister, Kaylee. Not my date! Not ever."

"Thanks for making it sound like the worst thing that could happen to anyone," Kaylee complains with a smile.

"Hey, if anyone suggested I was dating my little sister, I'd be less than thrilled, too."

"You have a little sister? What grade is she in? I'm in sixth. Maybe I know her."

"Yeah, you probably do. Her name is Jayla."

"Oh. Yeah. I do know her. She's funny like you." Kaylee blushes so quickly you'd think she'd just eaten one of Ricki's fries.

"Why, thank you. But I doubt she's *as* funny as me, but I'm sure she tries."

I look up at the clock on the wall. It took a lot longer to walk to town than I'd thought it would, and if we are going to beat Mom home, we need to leave. Now. "Wow, check out the time. Kaylee we have to go."

Kaylee looks up and sees the time and pops up out of her chair as if someone just yelled fire.

"Whoa, you must have something really good waiting for you at home," Ricki laughs.

"Not quite. We have to make it home before our mother does. This was an unapproved excursion. We get tired of leftover pasta in the fridge." Crap. Why did I have to run off at the mouth?

"Dang. My mother never makes pasta. You can call me over to do away with the leftovers anytime."

"Deal," I say as I push my chair back. "See ya."

"Yep. That you will." Ricki lifts another less-soaked fry and waves it in the air. "See you too, Kaylee."

"Bye. It was nice to meet you."

As soon as we get out the door, I walk-run down the street. Kaylee lags and drags behind. Does she want us to get caught?

"Come on, Kale. We have to hurry."

"I'm trying. My stomach is full of French fries." Her long, slow legs move a little faster. We make it back to the house at ten to seven. About thirty seconds after I sit down in front of the TV, Mom comes in the front door.

"Hello, anybody home?" Can you tell she and Kaylee are related?

"In here, Mom," Kaylee calls out.

She heads right for the kitchen where Kaylee is studiously hunched over her math book. I guess she knows where she can find me.

"Oh, good job, Kaylee, you're doing your homework."

I hear her open the fridge where she must be staring at the mayonnaise as well because I don't hear the door close.

"Haven't you kids had dinner yet? The pasta is still here."

Uh ohhh. I head into the kitchen before Kaylee has a chance to answer, but she beats me to the punch.

"We had a bunch of snacks, Mom. We weren't really hungry."

Mom sees me in the doorway. "Oh, there you are. Hi, honey. A bunch of snacks, huh? I'll warm this up. We can eat together. I'm starving."

Kaylee looks at me as if she is going to die. "Oh, that's okay, Mom, I'm still not very hungry."

Mom pulls the bowl of pasta out of the fridge and puts it on the counter. "You have to eat some dinner, Kale. I don't want you kids snacking throughout the afternoon if you aren't going to be able to eat something healthy."

I shrug and go back to the TV room. Kaylee follows. She elbows me in the ribs and whispers in desperation, "If I have to eat one bite of pasta I am going to puke all over the table!"

"Well, don't puke on my plate."

Kaylee clutches her stomach and sits down beside me on the couch.

"He's really nice," she whispers. "You're lucky. At least you have a friend."

I want to tell her that it doesn't feel like Ricki is a friend yet, but I don't want to say it out loud. I don't want to wreck the feeling inside that he is.

#

"A family meeting? What does that even mean?" I ask on our way home from school.

"I don't know. Mom was acting kind of weird this morning. Maybe she and Dad are going to announce that they want to get back together again. Maybe they realized divorce isn't what they thought it would be and they want us to be a family again."

I hate the way Kaylee goes right to hopeful fantasy. "Yeah, cause haven't you noticed how often they spend time together, and how hard it is to use the phone to call all our friends cause Mom and Dad are chatting happily together every time we try?"

Hopeful slides down Kaylee's face and onto the ground where my words trample and flatten it onto the sidewalk.

I keep my head down and notice the drag of Kaylee's red high tops on the cement. Does she know that her left big toe has begun to wear a little hole into the tip of her shoe?

I go straight to my room when we get home. I emptied the tower of boxes in the corner. I surrendered to the truth of my parents' divorce and put my things on the walls and shelves. Not putting them out didn't change the situation, so what's the point in that?

Dad hasn't been to the house to see my room. He hasn't been in my room since we moved here months ago.

I pick Zorba up off of my side table. I reread the bit where he answers the Book Worm about being married: "Am I not a man? And is a man not stupid? I'm a man, so I married. Wife, children, house, everything. The full catastrophe."

I wonder if Zorba means that all men who marry are stupid. Or is it marriage and family that's stupid? I wonder if

Dad agrees with Zorba about marriage and children. Does he see himself as a stupid man? Were we the "full catastrophe" he had to endure?

I put the book down again and go downstairs. Zorba the Greek can be very confusing at times.

Kaylee's in the kitchen. "Anything other than pasta in the fridge?" I wonder if she will take the olive branch. Her flowered overalls have little threads hanging off where she cut them into shorts. She hates throwing them away, so she just turns the pants into shorts when she grows out of them. I'm about to say something about the little threads but see the olive branch go up in flames and decide better of it.

The phone saves me from myself and my sarcasm. "I got it."

"Hello?"

"Hi Flip. It's Mom. It looks like I'm not going to be able to come home early for our family meeting after all. Serena called in sick so I have to take her shift. I spoke to your father already."

"Ok. What's this family meeting about anyways, Mom?" There's a long pause which makes me sorry I asked the question. I give the short hairs around my ears a hard tug.

"Look, Flip, your friend Harley from Sea Trek was my first client the other day. We had a nice chat. When he discovered I was your mother, our nice chat wasn't so nice anymore. You and Kaylee have a lot of explaining to do."

"Oh," is the best I can come out with under the circumstances.

"I will talk to your father and we will reschedule our meeting."

"Ok," is the next best thing that comes out of my mouth. "Bye, Mom."

"Who was it, Flip?" Kaylee calls from the kitchen. Maybe she senses the sizzle in the air.

"Oh boy," I say as I head back to the kitchen. "Oh boy, oh boy, oh boy."

Kaylee has her back to me but spins around quickly on my third "oh boy."

"What the heck, Flip? What are you 'oh boying' about?'"

She looks at my face, or maybe it's the handful of hair I've practically ripped out of my head, and says, "Uh oh? What happened, Flip?"

"Oh boy, we are in a heap of trouble. Mom knows about our taking the kayak out of the lagoon."

"*What? How?* How could she know? I didn't say a word to anyone. I swear. How could she know?"

"Harley was one of her clients the other day. I guess she was talking to him about her wonderful, trustworthy children who just love going to Schoonmacher to paddle around the little lagoon. Harley probably said, 'Oh, which little angels are yours?' And, you know, Mom said – 'Well, Flip and Kaylee' and the rest you can figure out yourself."

"Oh boy. I can definitely figure out the rest of that conversation." She lowers her voice to sound like Harley. "Yes, your dear children actually took one of our kayaks out onto the Richardson Bay knowing they weren't allowed and then almost got blown all the way to San Francisco but were luckily rescued by one of our trusty employees who happened to tell me all about it."

"That sounds about right," I sit down at the kitchen table with my head in my hands. Kaylee sits down beside me.

"Do you think they found out about Zorba, too?"

"Zorba? No. Why would they? No one knows about us and Zorba."

"Except that woman with the dog," Kaylee reminds me. "Maybe she's one of Mom's clients as well. Sausalito is a lot smaller than San Francisco. Maybe everyone here knows each other's business."

I shake my head, hoping that by doing so I will wipe out any chance of that notion being true. "I doubt it."

"Did she say what time the meeting is?"

"No, she had to cancel it. She's coming home late. She already called Dad. God he's going to be so disappointed in me."

"In us."

"Yeah, but more in me. I'm the one who talked you into going out. I'm the older brother."

"I'm not going to rat you out, Flip. I promise."

I look at my sister. Sometimes I forget we aren't related by blood.

"I'm going to my room," she says. Worry is draped so heavily over her shoulders that her back is curved under its weight.

"I'm sorry, Kale. It's my fault."

"Whatever," she says. "It doesn't matter anymore whose fault it is. We're in this mess together now." She turns to look at me. I don't know how a smile can find its way across such a sad face, but hers does. She slumps out the door, her unbuttered toast sits on a plate waiting for its jam.

I notice the note Mom left this morning. *Hey kids. I'll be home around 5pm. Your dad will be here as well. Please have your homework finished. Your dad will pick up a pizza on his way home.*

I'm almost sad the family meeting is called off. I could have shown Dad my room, and we'd get pizza for dinner for a change.

I turn the paper over and pick up the pen. I have no idea who I'm writing to until the pen begins to move like fingers on a Ouji board.

Dear Zorba,

The knot has come undone. But the rope has turned into a noose. I wish I knew what to do now. What would you do? You'd turn the noose into a rope swing, I bet. I don't know how to do that. I want you to teach me.

Mom and Dad schedule our family meeting for the next day. Kaylee and I come home straight after school. I've had plenty of time to think about all the ways my parents are going to be all sorts of angry with me. I haven't come up with a good excuse for my behavior. I know that's what my mother will ask for: "What do you have to say for yourself young man?"

I have nothing to say for myself. But I'd like to ask them what they have to say for themselves. I'd like to ask them where they think they get off splitting up our family, taking us away from the only home and friends we've ever had, and turning my world so upside down that I no longer know where I fit in with my family, in my school, or in my very own skin. I'd like to know what excuse they have for that.

My clock says 5 pm when the first car pulls into the driveway. The somersaults that are going on in my belly make it hard for me to move to the window. It's not Mom. It's Dad getting out of his truck. Mom pulls into the driveway right behind him. Oh man, they're both coming in at the same time?

"Hello? Kaylee? Flip?" Mom calls out. Dad says nothing.

"We're in here," Kaylee answers.

I hear someone come down the hall towards the room. "Where?" It's my dad. I'm relieved.

"In here, Dad."

He stands in the doorway to Kaylee's room and looks around for a minute. "Wow pumpkin, you really did a good job decorating your room."

He's not mad. It's Dad. He doesn't get mad about stuff like this. I move my body close to his, hoping for a hug. Kaylee does the same.

Group hug, I think to myself and almost smile.

But the sharpness of Mom's voice cuts through any hope of relief. "Let's move this into the living room."

We've barely made it to the den before Mom turns on me, "Would you like to explain?"

I'd like to say, "No thanks. I'd rather not," but that's not a good idea. I look at the floor.

"I don't know why we did it. It was my idea. I wanted to go out to see the houseboats. We'd paddled a ton of times in the lagoon and I thought we were ready."

"I told you specifically before you left *not* to go out of the lagoon, Flip." Mom's brown hair falls into her eyes. She practically rips it out by the roots as she combs it back out of her face.

"Let's give him a second to explain, Sheila." Dad sounds angry. He's taken a seat on the couch. Kaylee is beside him.

I need to stand. I look down at my bare feet. I have Native American feet. They're wide, thick and flat. My toes are short and stubby. I'd like to study them a bit longer.

"I know Mom told us not to go out. It was a dumb idea. I was mad because I wasn't going to be able to see you on Wednesdays because of baseball practice. I just didn't care about anything, or anyone."

"Including your little sister?" Mom's words are thorny. She sprays them up and down my body when she speaks. "You kids could have been hurt. In fact, your sister *was* hurt!"

"It's not all his fault. I went along, too. I didn't refuse to go. I'm old enough to say no if I want to." Kaylee's overalls are too big. They make her look like she's half her age. Her face is bright red, and, of course, she looks like she's going to cry. In this moment, though, she is my best friend. I can count on her, no matter what. Her words give me strength.

"I'm sorry. I know what we did was wrong." I look directly into my father's cloudy blue eyes.

He's disappointed in me. I knew it.

"Flip, I know how hard this move and our separation has been for you. For all of us. And I understand your anger. But it seems you are blaming your mother for what happened between us, and that's not right. Your mother and I made this decision together. It's no one's fault."

I look over at Mom. I see the sadness fill her eyes as she nods her head. She must have told Dad that I've been mad or something. Although I don't know how she'd even know I am since she's hardly ever home.

"I'm not blaming Mom." My words gush from my mouth and splatter on the floor between us. "I blame both of you. You didn't try hard enough. You didn't care enough about Kaylee and me to make it work. That's messed up, and I blame you both for it."

I regret my words before they even finish spilling from my mouth. I wish I could suck them back in. Instead, I cover them quickly in a whisper. "I'm sorry, Dad. I miss you. I don't want you to be disappointed in me."

Mom says something softly but I can't hear. Kaylee gets up and gives Mom a hug. I'm confused.

"We do care about disappointing you, too," Kaylee wraps her arms around Mom, her eyes shooting darts at me.

"Not only did you endanger both of your lives, but you both lied repeatedly to your mother and to the people at Sea Trek. I am sorely disappointed in you both." Even though he says he's disappointed in both of us, his words are meant for me. Each one of them has my name on it and hits me on my chest like a boulder shot from a cannon.

"We need to figure out how we're going to deal with this now." Dad isn't happy with all the tears and sad feelings, I can tell.

"There's no point in grounding them from Sea Trek." Mom perks up a little with the idea of a punishment. "Harley says you haven't been back since your last little escapade." She pauses before pulling the pin from the grenade and tossing it into the room. "What I want to know," her voice picks up speed and volume, "is how many other things have you lied about? How many times have you left this house telling me you're going one place while ending up in another?"

My heart sinks. I lock my eyes onto the leg of my mother's chair and wait for Kaylee to spill the Zorba beans all over the floor. The room begins to shrink. My heartbeat pounds against the walls. No one seems to notice. When the pounding stops, the quiet pushes up against the walls until Dad's voice steps into the silence. "You kids have really broken your mother's trust." Disappointment is attached to every word. Dad looks tired. He's grown old, and there's no light left in his eyes. We don't make him happy the way we used to. "We need to know that we can trust you kids, Flip. We need to count on that."

I look over towards Kaylee. Her face is a blank white sheet. She's leaning in to Mom's side. "It won't happen again, Dad." I'm talking to Dad, but I'm looking at Mom. Why am I doing that?

"You kids go on back to your rooms. I want to talk with your father for a few minutes."

I'm desperate to say something else to make it right. I *can't* leave the room until I make this right.

"Flip, go with your sister. Your mother and I are going to talk."

Kaylee has left the room already. I didn't even see her go. "Okay, Dad."

Kaylee waits for me in front of her bedroom door and whispers, "We should have told them, but I don't want them to tell us we can't go visit him."

Kaylee sighs and shrugs her shoulders when I don't respond. We walk into our rooms and close our doors behind us. I expect to hear them yell. I wait for the slam of the front door. Instead, there's a knock at my door.

"Come in," I stand up.

"I'm leaving now, Flip. I'll see you and your sister on Wednesday."

He walks over to me and puts his arm around my shoulder and gives me a light squeeze. Then he turns and leaves my room.

He doesn't even stop to notice the posters on the walls.

I wait for the sound of his car in the driveway. I peek out the window and see Mom has to move her car so he can get out of the driveway.

They don't hug goodbye or wave to each other. They just get in their separate cars and move out of each other's way.

CHAPTER SIX

Practice is cancelled today. Teacher conferences. I shift in my seat waiting for the hands on the wall clock to move.

"*Oye Felipe. Calmate hombre,*" Ricki whispers.

"Huh?" I never have a clue what he's saying to me in Spanish. He doesn't care. He thinks because I look Latino I should be able to speak Spanish. I never cared about speaking Spanish before, but now I wish I did.

"I said calm your butt down, dude. You look like you've got *frijoles saltarines* in your pants."

"*Frijoles* what? Beans in my pants? Dude, that's nasty."

"Mexican jumping beans? You know the ones that jump when you put them in the sun."

The bell rings before I have time to ask. "I have no idea what you're talking about, but I gotta go."

"*Bueno,*" he waves as I jump like a bean out of my seat. "Where are you going in such a hurry? We don't have practice today. You wanna go to town for something to eat?"

Damn! I want to do something with Ricki after school, but I haven't seen Dad since last Wednesday.

"Not today. I gotta do something with my dad today."

"Okay amigo. Hasta mañana."

"Yeah, see you tomorrow." I do know some Spanish.

Dad's truck sits in the circle along with a dozen other cars. It looks like a used car lot. My dad's truck is more used than the others. The green paint on his Nissan pickup has a thousand rust spots and dents. I circle around to the passenger side door and pop my head in the window.

"Arggggh." He jumps so high his head hits the roof of the truck. "My god, Flip, you want to give me a heart attack?"

I climb in and give him a hug. He wraps his arms around me and then gives me a slap on the back. "So, how was school?"

"The same, Dad, always the same. No friends, no fun. Except maybe Ricki. You know, the Guatemalan guy on the team?"

"Yeah. He's got a sister Kaylee's age, right?"

"Yeah."

There's a moment of quiet, then Dad asks, "How's Zorba?" I almost jump out of my seat. "Have you read any further?"

"Oh. Yeah. Yes, I have. Zorba's like a little kid with big feelings who's not afraid to show them." I think about how Dad isn't like that. How when he's mad he "takes a time out" instead of sticking around and fighting it out. Or how when he's sad, or we're sad, he makes a joke and tries to distract us. "When Zorba gets mad, or happy, or sad, he dances. He jumps around like a crazy man or cries like a baby."

"Yes, I love that about Zorba. He'll dance his way through his most joyful moments and sink down low and deep in the hard times. He cherishes every bit of life."

"He's a little crazy too, though." I have been reading bits and pieces of the book. The similarities between our Zorba and Zorba the Greek are scary. "The guy cut his own finger off because it got in the way when he was doing pottery. *Who does* something like that? That's insanity, Dad."

"Ahh, yes. I forgot about that part. Zorba's a man of passion, not reason. He's impulsive and focused at the same time. That's why the Book Worm loves him so much. He wishes he could find his own passion, although, I'm sure he'd like to keep all his fingers."

"Yeah, I see that. I like the way he thinks. Like when the Book Worm asks Zorba why he should take him along with him, and Zorba yells, 'Why, why? Can't a man do anything without a why?'"

"Yes, that's it, exactly. He doesn't want to question every little thing. He just wants to live life in the moment, according to whatever mood he's in. Wouldn't that be a wonderful way to go through life?"

Before I can answer, Kaylee rips the car door open so hard I think it's going to come off its hinges.

"Go, just go," she's crying. She pushes my seat forward and tries to squeeze into the back.

"Jeeze, Kale, chill. Let me get the seat forward so you can get in for pizza's sake."

"Hurry up, just do it."

"Kale, honey, what's going on? What's the matter?"

Dad reaches back to put his hand on her. She pushes it away. Apparently, my sister has *no* problem living life in the moment according to what her mood is.

A couple of kids walk by the car. There's a red head with braids and a blond guy with a backwards baseball cap. The red head calls out, "Bye Kaylee," and lifts her hand in a short, half circle wave.

Kaylee sinks down in her seat.

"What the heck happened to you?" That came out meaner than I meant it to.

"They were making fun of my overalls. Dad, will you just go!"

Dad pulls the truck from the circle. "What happened, sweetheart?"

"A boy in class asked me why I wear the same clothes every day." Kaylee uses her shirt sleeve to wipe her eyes and nose. Gross.

"What'd you tell him?" I ask.

"I said I liked them. He looked over at his friends across the room and shrugged. They all laughed. They were laughing at me!"

"Oh honey, you can't be sure they were laughing at you." Dad looks at Kaylee in the rearview mirror.

He's wrong, of course. They were laughing at her. I want to be on Kaylee's side, but she's in sixth grade. It's time for her to change her look.

"But that's not the worst part. Levi came over to say goodbye and I pushed past him and huffed out of the room. Levi and Casie are the only two kids in the class I have any fun with.

Now he must think I'm crazy. I hate it here. I want to go back to the city." Kaylee sinks lower in the seat. I turn to face forward and wait.

"I'm sorry, Kale Bug. I know it's hard to start over. I'm sure it will all work out, honey."

Kale snorts from the back seat. Dad's eyes are glued to the yellow lines on the road. He has nothing more to say. So I will.

"Don't you think it's time to lose the overalls? I mean, they're not exactly a great fashion statement for sixth grade." I can't help it. I'm mad. She's ruining our Wednesday with Dad.

"Oh nice, Flip, really nice. I thought I could at least count on you to stick up for me. After all the times I've covered for you!"

Her foot rams the back of my seat so hard my body lurches forward. It's not the kick in the seat that bothers me. It's the look on Dad's face.

"Dang Kale, cool it. It was just a suggestion."

Then my father takes a hard left turn in the conversation, steering our mood to *happy land.* "So, how about some liquid cavities?"

I don't find the funny in our family description of ice cream right now. It screams pathetic cop-out to me. I look out the window. Antonio's riding his bike. His legs are moving fast. His huge grey backpack shifts from left to right. I want to call out to him, to ask him what he's doing this afternoon. But Antonio would rather stick his head in a mud puddle than hang out with me. And to tell you the truth, I'd like to be in that mud puddle with him right now.

We drive in silence until Dad makes another attempt. "Come on you guys, we have a whole afternoon together, let's have a good time."

"Yeah, sure Dad," I say. I look forward to being with my father all week. There'll be nothing left if this turns to donkey dung too.

"Fine," Kaylee mutters from the backseat. Kaylee has taken the screeching left turn away from her drama and onto *Family Fun Lane* along with Dad and me.

"Liquid cavities here we come." The appearance of family happiness is plastered pretty on our faces.

Our liquid cavity trip to Woody's lasts longer than usual. Dad runs into a friend from the city. They worked together in San Francisco. They talk about how little work there is.

Kaylee and I walk to the pet store to watch the kittens in the window. "I'm sorry I said what I did about your overalls, Kale."

"Whatever," she won't look at me. The reflection of her face in the store window says "I'm not ready to forgive you for this one."

Kaylee has gone along with my lies and sneaking out of the house when we should be home. She didn't squeal about our kayaking escapade, or tell anyone about Zorba. She takes my side when Mom jumps down my throat about the dishes in the sink, or laundry on the floor. She really has covered for me. I study her reflection in the pet shop window. She looks different. Her face is tight, and the corners of her mouth are turned down. We never talk about the divorce.

I want to make peace with her, but Dad calls us over before I have a chance.

Ms. Mason's voice buzzes like a mosquito in my ear. Everyone's pulling their social studies folders out of their desks. I shuffle through pages of crumpled notes, old homework, and god knows what else before I find my folder.

"Got it," I announce to no one in particular.

Ricki turns to see what I *got* and says, "Dang Flip – you better be careful when you stick your hand in that desk. There's no telling what you're going to find in there."

"Last week I found the gecko from the fourth grade class in here. She and her twelve babies were living in the three-story nest they'd built inside this desk."

Ricki laughs, "You going to practice today?"

"Yep. How 'bout you?"

"Oh yeah. It's the only reason I come to school – so I can play ball."

Not true! Ricki is one of the smartest kids I know, and he loves school.

"Did you speak Spanish when you came to this country?" Wow that was a curveball question.

"I probably knew Spanish when I was in the orphanage. I don't remember ever speaking it though. Were you born in this country, or in Guatemala?"

"I was born here. My parents left Guatemala towards the end of the civil war."

"Do you consider yourself Guatemalan or American?"

"I was born here, so I'm not Guatemalan. But I don't feel totally American either. I'm *Indígena*."

98

"*Indígena?*"

"Indigenous, Native American. Mayan, actually. What about you? Do you see yourself as Guatemalan or American?"

"I don't know. I guess both, or maybe neither. I think I act more like a kid from the United States than Guatemala. I don't really feel Guatemalan or Latino when I am around a bunch of Spanish-speaking kids."

"You're *indígena*, like me." Ricki thumps his chest with the palm of his hand. "Do you know which people are yours in Guatemala? You look like you're from the K'iche' like me."

"I have no idea. I don't know anything about my people, or my birth family."

I wonder if my parents know. Mom has mentioned having paperwork from the adoption. I haven't been interested. Being Flip Simpson, brother to Kaylee and son to Fenton and Sheila Simpson felt like enough. Now nothing feels the way it did.

For years I thought I was white like the rest of my family. I know that sounds ridiculous, but it's true. Looking into the light eyes and pale skin of my parents and sister colored the view I had of myself. Or maybe I should say, un-colored the view I had of myself. Until I was old enough to really understand race, I was certain I was the same as my family. Since we moved, I've noticed myself more. The way I move differently than anyone else in my family. My short legs don't cross a room the same way my father's long legs do. My smile doesn't reveal a picket fence of white; it's more like a wall of square white bricks. I'm a stranger everywhere I stand these days. At home, at school, even on the baseball field.

I look over at Ricki. He wears his K'iche' with such pride. I wish I could wear K'iche' the way a Native American wears Hopi Indian or Cherokee. I'd like to feel part of a tribe.

Ricki opens his pamphlet and looks at our assignment. I'm not done with this conversation. "How are families in Guatemala different than here? How do the K'iche' people live?"

"Well, there's a big difference between how the *Ladinos* in the cities live and how the Mayan families in the countryside live."

"What's a *Ladino*?"

"*Ladinos* are the people who even if they are indigenous don't practice the rituals and culture of the Maya. They live in the cities and dress like we do here. The K'iche' from the countryside are pure Mayan. They dress in traditional clothes and live from the land. They worship nature."

Ricki opens and closes the pamphlet as he speaks. "When we go back for holidays, it's crazy how many kids and cousins there are. Even a simple dinner becomes a huge *fiesta*. Everyone's always so happy to see my parents. The entire village shows up. My parents swear they're all family."

I think about my family, once four together, now down to three in two separate houses. I wonder if I have cousins or siblings in Guatemala. "Do you wish you lived there instead of here?"

"No. Not really. I like being with my cousins, but it doesn't *feel* like home to me. The people there are so poor. Not all the people, but many of them. My mom's family is from a place called Quetzaltenango. There are no malls, movie theaters, mini golf ranges. Life there is simple and hard.

Everyone works – even the young kids. I love going there, but I like coming home too."

I'm relieved by his answer.

"Ricki, Flip. Less talk, more reading, please," Ms. Mason calls out.

Ricki sits up. "*Hombre*, I told you. We're going to run out of time."

"You're right," I say. But my head isn't in the project. I'm thinking about Guatemala and the family I might have there.

#

On Thursday, I decide to take a trip to the public library. I can't get the word "K'iche'" out of my mind.

"Who are these Kitchies again? How are you related to them?" Thing Two is right beside me as we head for the Sausalito library. I try to explain what Ricki told me yesterday.

"In Guatemala, there are different tribes of Indians. Just like in this country. You know – like the Navajo Indians in Arizona. Or the Ohlone Indians from around here."

"So, you're Native American?" It sounds strange when she says it.

"Yep. I guess I am. Guatemala is a part of the Americas. Ricki calls us '*Indígena*.'"

"Indi – what?"

Kaylee doesn't have a good ear for languages. Mom says I do because I heard mostly Spanish the first year of my life.

"*Indígena*. It means indigenous, or native. Native American, see?"

"Oh. Cool. I thought you were Guatemalan."

"I was born in Guatemala, but I'm not really Guatemalan. I'm American. I want to see pictures of the K'iche'. Maybe I look like them. Maybe they really are my people."

"Hey! I thought we were your people." I look to see if she's kidding. She's not. Worry walks across Kaylee's forehead. I watch as it makes a trail from her eyebrows to the corners of her eyes.

"Of course, you're my people. I'm just curious about my heritage."

"I get it," she says. But I notice Worry hasn't walked off her face yet. Kaylee heads for the children's section of the library to look for another James Herriot book.

Wikipedia rocks. It takes me thirty seconds to find information on the K'iche' Indians of Guatemala.

"According to the 2011 census, K'iche' people constituted 11% of the Guatemalan population. The large majority of K'iche' people live in the highlands of Guatemala. Most K'iche' speak their native language and have at least a working knowledge of Spanish. Maya languages closely related to K'iche' are Uspantek, Sakapultek, Kaqchikel, and Tzutujil.

I scroll down even further to find a photo of a woman with a baby tied to her back in a colorful cloth. I've seen photos like this before. Mom and Dad used to have books about Guatemala on our living room table. I wonder who got them, Mom or Dad. Sometimes I feel like my life is a math equation of fractions: A whole family, cut in half, but divided into thirds. And then there's the Guatemalan part of the equation. What fraction of my Guatemalan family am I? How many parts to their whole are there? And how do I factor that part of who I am into the equation?

The next photo is of a woman sitting on the ground cross-legged, surrounded by fruits and vegetables. She's sorting through a stack of long stemmed flowers. Over her shoulder, a little face peeks out from behind. I can't tell if it's a girl or a boy, but I recognize the straight black hair and the almond eyes as my own.

I search for "Quetzaltenango." Photos of people I assume are the K'iche' pop up on the screen. I zoom in on a few of the male faces in a crowd of people scattered up and down the stone steps of a church. A kid about my age stands next to an older woman. He has my nose, my round face, and square teeth. I jump up from the computer and find Kaylee.

"Hey, come look at this," I whisper loudly.

"Shhhh. Okay, I'm coming." Kaylee's afraid of getting yelled at in the library.

I point at the photo, still magnified on the screen. "Who does that remind you of?"

"Whoa. He could be your brother. That's amazing. Where is that? What are they doing?"

I de-magnify the photo and scroll down. *"It's Market Day in Quetzaltenango. People are gathering to sell."*

I look at Kaylee. She's looking at me. Now Curious is crossing her face.

I smile. "Pretty cool, huh?"

"Yeah. Pretty cool. But what are you looking for?"

What *am* I looking for? I came here to find out about the K'iche' of Guatemala. I'm looking for more than that now. "I don't know. I'm just interested in where I came from."

"Cool," she says. "I'm going to go back to the other room. Tell me when you're done. I've got a few books I want to check out."

Kaylee walks away. I stare at the boy in the photo. I'm certain Ricki is right. My people are K'iche'.

CHAPTER SEVEN

"Great catch, Flip. You've got the makings of a pro. Okay guys, bring it in." Coach Erik is nothing like Coach Dave. First of all, Coach Dave wouldn't single me out for a good play the way Coach Erik does. Coach Dave knows better than to make one player more important than the others.

The Willow Tree Academy Team for Beginners is *nothing* like my team in San Francisco. It's more like a substitute for PE than a baseball league, which is why it's so strange that my teammates get so bent out of shape by my game.

"Great catch, Simpson. I see a place on the Giants for you." I look over at Antonio. The way his lip curls over his teeth makes me want to suggest he get a rabies vaccine.

"Yeah, but I'm not sure *bat boy* is his dream position," Damian adds.

Damian and Antonio are like Click and Clack the Tappet Brothers. Click and Clack have a car talk show on the radio every Saturday morning. Dad and I used to listen to it all the time.

"Well, at least that way he can look up and wave to the two of you. You'll have no trouble finding them among the fans, Flip. They'll be the two yahoos yelling, "Peanuts, popcorn, get your cotton candy here.""

All three of us laugh with Ricki. He's got his cap on sideways and his pants pulled up above his belly button. "Come on, Babe Ruth, let's go to town and get an ice cream or something."

"Great. Cool. Awesome." Did I really just say that?

"*Andale pues, vamanos.*"

Andale pues, vamanos, means something like – "All right then. Let's go." Ricki mixes English and Spanish like my mother mixes peanut butter with jelly.

"Isn't your mom picking you up after practice?" I ask.

"Not today. She just got a part-time job with the Canal Community Alliance. I'm taking the bus home now."

"What's the Canal Community Alliance?"

"I'll tell you on the way."

I grab my backpack and glove. I don't fail to notice Click and Clack following Ricki and me with hungry eyes. Hungry because Ricki is one of those guys who most everyone wishes they were friends with. Ricki wears *cool* like a three-piece suit. The kind of formal that says, "I'm going places." At the same time, he'll have you bent over double with his wisecracks.

I bet he invited me to go to town to show Click and Clack that he's got my back.

"Don't take those two *burros* too seriously. They're just *celoso*. You've got some mean talent on the field, Flip. It's a shame it's being wasted on the school team."

I wish I knew what *celoso* meant, but I'm not going to highlight my lousy Spanish skills right now. "What's up with the Willow Tree team? How come they don't play other schools more often?"

"We're a public charter school. There's not a lot of extra money to put into building a league team."

"Huh," I can't say much about this because I have no idea what a public charter school is. I don't want Ricki to know that though.

Ice cream in town with Ricki feels like winning the lottery. We talk about baseball and throw the ball in the park downtown. I never worried about looking stupid with my friends in the city. I could just be me. I know Ricki isn't taking notes on all the ways I'm a doofus, but I keep watch of what I say and how I respond even so.

"The Canal Community Alliance is an organization that helps the Latino families in San Rafael who need jobs, or food, or legal help. Stuff like that." We're walking back towards the school and the bus stop for San Rafael.

"Where does the *Canal* come into it?"

"The Canal is a section of San Rafael that is mostly Latino. The stores are all run by Latinos, and most everyone you meet speaks Spanish. It's Marin County's south of the border."

"Sounds like the Mission District in San Francisco."

"*Si. Exacto.* You should come to my house one day. You'd feel right at home there."

I'm not sure what he means by that. Right at home with his family? Right at home in the Canal? "That'd be cool." I resist the urge to ask what day and what time. I don't want him to think I'm desperate. Which of course, I am!

107

"Only one week left till summer. What are you doing?"

I'm embarrassed to tell him that my parents have signed us up for camp because they don't want Kaylee and me roaming around the streets of Sausalito on our own. "I'm not sure yet. What about you?"

Ricki stops in front of the Golden Gate Transit sign. "We're going to Guatemala for three weeks to visit *mi familia*. After that, not much."

"Are you going to Quetzaltenango?"

"Wow, you remembered the name. Impressive. Yeah, we're staying with my Tia and her kids. Maybe I should see if I can find some of your *familia* while I'm there?"

"Oh. Huh." My thoughts and my words have tied themselves into a knot. Find my family? It sounds so simple when Ricki says it. What should I say?

Here ya go, Ricki, here's the names of my birth parents – Isabela and Miguel Menchu. Or maybe it's Yolanda and Javier Rios. Give them my love and tell them to send a photo of themselves and any siblings I might have.

The knot wraps itself around my wanting and the fear of asking. I think about Dad and the look of disappointment in his eyes the other day. Or Mom sitting across from him with Kaylee's arms around her, assuring her that we did care about disappointing her. What would they think if I suddenly took an interest in knowing my birth family? What would it mean about my love for them? About my place in the crumbling structure of our family?

"Thanks for the offer. I'm not sure I could find their names at this point. Maybe another time, though."

"Okay. *Esta bien.* Here's where the bus to south of the border picks me up. I'll see you tomorrow."

"Okay. See ya."

Ricki's offer jumps in front of me on the walk home. I push, kick, and scream it aside. It persists.

What? What do you want with me? I can't do this right now. I can't think about another family I know nothing about. I'm busy. Leave me alone. Can't you see I've got problems with my own family?

My own family. What does that mean? Aren't they both my *own family? Mi familia?* The equation has become whole. The fraction is simple. One half. One half of my family is here in the States, the other half in Guatemala. I shove the thoughts aside with more conviction. I think about going home to the TV and Kaylee. Being with Ricki has reminded me of how much I miss my friends in the city. I've had a bite of the friendship pie after months of starvation. It's almost worse having had the taste of it again and wondering if there's any more where it came from.

#

Of course, I forget to call home to tell Kaylee I was hanging out with Ricki after practice. Kaylee's way of holding on to our missing mother is to become her. "Where have you been, Flip? I thought practice ends at four? It's 5:30 already."

"Okay, *Mom.* Sorry I didn't call and let you know my every move." Kaylee doesn't just *become* Mom, she *is* Mom. The way she stands and the sound of her voice. Even the slight tilt of her head when she grills me – it's all Mom. I am not like these people – my family. My body and my gestures come from a different genetic pool.

Kaylee looks at the corner of the hall carpet as if there were crickets coming out from under it. "I just didn't know where you were. You always come home after practice, that's all."

I guess she was pretty lonely here at the house by herself. "Ricki asked me to go for ice cream after practice."

"Oh, wow. That's cool. At least you have a friend now." She doesn't say it in a jealous sort of way. She's happy for me, I can tell.

"Yeah. It only took a few months. Where's Casie these days?"

"She's got stuff she has to do after school most days."

"Oh bummer. You wanna go see Zorba tomorrow?"

She smiles big. "Yeah, great."

#

We haven't gone to see Zorba in a while. I'm looking forward to seeing him. The fog is thick today. The docks are wet, and the air is heavy. Zorba's door and window are shut.

We're gonna have to go inside if we want to see him." Kaylee's not asking, she's telling.

"I know. I just wonder if today is a 'good day' or not."

"We'll find out soon enough." It's weird how Kaylee becomes so bold and sure when she's around Zorba. I feel like the earth is spinning off its axis when we're with Zorba. It's as if the rules and regulations to a game I've known my whole life have changed, and I've been thrown into it not knowing how to meet the pitch. With Zorba as pitcher, it's impossible to prepare for what's coming over the plate.

Kaylee doesn't hesitate. She walks the plank towards the Good Ship's front door. Right before her foot hits the deck of the boat, Kaylee slips on the wet surface of the wood. Her feet go out from under her and she lands on her butt with a shriek.

Zorba is out the door and by her side before me. "Well now, Humpty Dumpty – you've had quite a fall, haven't you? Has your shell been cracked? Can we put you back together again?"

Kaylee laughs and wipes the tears off her face. "I'm okay. It's as slippery as ice."

"Shall we come in off the ice and out of the frain?"

"Frain?" I ask.

"Yes, Boss. Its frogging frain."

"That's fog and rain combined, right, Zorba?" Kaylee's proud of herself for figuring it out before me.

"Yes, my little scholar. That's exactly what it is. Let's take cover. You ready to board the Good Ship, Boss?"

I look into his eyes. They're not darting about, but they're not steady and calm either. I swear they're a bit darker than they were the last time we were here.

"I'm ready," I say.

Zorba's wearing a pair of red baggy pants and a rainbow scarf today. His orange sweater with purple swirls has lost its spring and hangs off of his body like a shower curtain. I wonder if that's what happened to my parents' marriage – if it lost its spring and hung heavy around them. It occurs to me that Zorba may be sneaking into some home on the hill here in Sausalito, going from room to room picking out fabrics to sew together to wear as pants, shirts, and scarves.

"Come on, Boss, I want to close the door. The damp is going to sink the ship if you don't hurry up. You can sew the stories that cloud your mind together inside just as easily as out."

Holy cow. He did it again. I'm going to have to be more careful about what I think around Zorba.

Once inside, it takes a minute for my eyes to adjust. The one and only light is covered over with Zorba's tie dye shirt. I wonder what he's wearing under his sweater.

Kaylee whistles, spinning slowly in a circle where she stands. I follow her gaze and then I see what she sees.

Lollipops. Hundreds of them hanging on the walls. There are small pops and big ones – like the kind you win at the county fair, which your parents threaten to remove from your room after three straight days of licking with no end in sight. "You'll be sucking on that for the better half of a year. One more day then you need to turn it in," they say.

"Wow," Kaylee says and then she begins to giggle. Not a little giggle. She's going on as if someone was tickling her. Is Crazy contagious? Could Kaylee be catching whatever Zorba has? I watch as my sister laughs and spins. I don't know if Crazy is contagious, but Kaylee's laughter is. Zorba begins to laugh as well. His eyes close and his mouth like a cave opens wide and dark inside. Zorba stops laughing for one second. He lowers his head, opens one eye and looks at me. Then he closes his eye again and throws his head back, laughing even louder.

It's as if he tickled my ribs with his one-eyed gaze. I don't decide to laugh, laughter creeps in to my chest and then, like a horse leaving the gate, bursts out of my mouth. Everything around us disappears. There's nothing – an endless sensation of funny that rushes through our bodies like a fountain. It's the best feeling in the world, as good as hitting a home run in the last inning to win the game. It's explosive and alive.

I don't know whose fountain runs out first, Zorba's maybe. The laughter begins to trickle, and then there's quiet.

"Well now, that was a delightful little belly scratch," Zorba says as he wipes the tears from his eyes with his scarf. He then offers an end to Kaylee who takes it and wipes her eyes as well. Next, they'll be blowing their noses in the thing!

"Where'd you get all these lollipops, Zorba?"

"Here and there."

"Is this how the Good Ship got her name?" Kaylee is still a bit winded from her giggling sprint.

"Not exactly, Alice in Wonderland. My mother named this holy vessel. She loved Shirley Temple, and she loved lollipops. Whenever she'd disappear and leave me alone, she'd always come back with a lollipop so that I'd forgive her for leaving. I just keep buying them. I guess I'm still trying to forgive her for never coming back the last time she left me."

The echo of laughter stops swirling around the room. It falls to the floor like ashes. I try to imagine what it would be like to have my mother or father leave home for the day, never to return. I miss my dad, but at least I know he's still there if I want to talk to him. Poor Zorba. How does one keep going after that kind of loss? No wonder he lives in a fairytale world.

Zorba walks over to the wall and takes down two medium-sized lollipops. He hands one to each of us. "You came back to me, so it's only proper that you each get a lollipop."

"Thanks," we say at the same time.

Zorba's boat is tidy in a way that surprises me. Things are lined up perfectly along the shelves. His books are stacked neatly in a corner, each binding perfectly in line with the other. I thought his home would be as chaotic as his mind, or as messy as his clothes.

"Have a seat," he points to the couch covered in what looks like someone's living room rug.

"Your home is so pretty," Kaylee says.

"Well thank you, Lady Luck. I like a tidy ship, you know. Can't have cobwebs and chaos seeping out of my head and into my home, now can I? Tell me now, have you tackled the tangles and untied the knots yet?" His eyes brush past Kaylee's and settle in behind my own.

"Well, not exactly. The knots are untied but we didn't find the loose spots. Someone else untied them for us."

Zorba nods. "Just as well. It doesn't matter how they come undone, just so long as they do."

I think about the disappointment in my father's eyes, and in a flash, an idea screams across my mind. *It might not have been you who turned out his light. The light might have gone out before the knot came undone.*

I look at Zorba. He smiles and nods ever so slightly. Did he just say that? In my mind? I decide to find out.

"What else could it be? How does one's light get turned out?" I watch Zorba carefully after asking the question aloud. I feel Kaylee's eyes on me, questioning. Zorba answers before she has time to speak.

"Listen, Boss, you can't take the light out of someone else's lamp. Only they can do that. You might be able to screw the bulb loose a little, causing their light to flicker, but we all decide when and whether we want to tighten the bulb and let our light shine."

"What are you two talking about?" Kaylee sounds annoyed.

"We're talking about watching someone you love struggle with their own sadness, and the ways we think we are responsible for their happiness. Right, Boss?"

"Yeah. But when we disappoint someone we love, isn't that the reason their light begins to dim?"

"Nope, nope, nope," Zorba's head moves from side to side with each "nope." "You can't disappoint me if I don't let you. It's only when we expect people to behave a certain way and they don't that we become disappointed. But who are we to expect people to be the way we decide they should? Nope, nope, nope. You are just being you, and there's nothing disappointing about that."

I shake my head. I know that what he's saying is true, but I can't figure out exactly how it applies to the situation with my dad.

"Shall we listen to some music?" He doesn't wait for an answer. He turns and walks towards the wall with dozens of record albums, the old-fashioned kind, neatly lined along the shelf. He runs his pinky along the records from left to right, "A is for Abba, D for Dylan, F is for Frampton, P is for Pink Floyd. Ahh yes, here she is. T for Temple. Shirley, dear."

Zorba has his records in alphabetical order of course. He puts the disc on the turntable and drops the needle down onto the record. The needle bounces and scratches along the record. It makes a horrible sound.

My father has a turntable as well. He loves his old records. I can tell you this, he never drops the needle arm onto any of his records!

The music is loud. "Someday I'm going to fly. I'll be a pilot too. And when I do, how would you, like to be my crew? On the Good Ship Lollipop. It's a sweet trip to the candy shop, where bon-bons play, on the sunny beach of Peppermint Bay."

Zorba sings along with the words. "Sings" might not be the right word. He's screaming the words out. When the verse is over, he picks the needle up again and drops it onto the record. Like magic, the needle skids across the surface and lands in the exact same place. Zorba extends his arms like we did when we were little, pretending to be a plane. Kaylee does the same, and off they go – flying around the room. When it comes to the line, "On the Good Ship Lollipop," Kaylee screams along with Zorba.

"Hey Zorba, aren't your neighbors going to complain?" I shout. "Zorba!"

"What? What's that you say?" He goes to lift the arm off the record. "I couldn't hear a word you said. Why aren't you dancing with us? Got rocks in your shoes? Cement in your soul? Come on, Boss, spread your wings and fly."

He drops the needle onto the record again, and sure enough, it lands in the same place. I watch them spin and dance until I can't stand it anymore. Zorba sees me walking towards the door and stops spinning. He lifts the needle from the record and spins around to face me.

"Where you off to, Boss? It ain't no party without you."

"I know. I'm sorry. It's just too loud."

"Too loud? Music can't be too loud. It enters your soul and lifts your spirits. The louder it is, the higher you go. You need to unload some of the boulders that weigh you down. You have to let life lift you and take you away. Away from this planet and all her troubles. Give yourself a break. You deserve it."

Zorba may be crazy, but what he's saying makes sense to me. I know he's right. I just don't know how to unload the boulders.

"Tell ya what, Boss, you choose next. What would you like to do?"

"I dunno, Zorba. I really don't." I move to the couch and sit. I feel like a loser. "I'm sorry to be such a party pooper."

"Tell us a story, Zorba." Kaylee has caught her breath.

"A story is it? How does that suit you, Boss?"

"Great. Fine. Tell us a story." I'm grateful for Kaylee's soaring spirit.

"A story it is. Let me put on my story-telling clothes." Zorba moves to a cupboard in the corner of the room. He opens the door that hangs off one hinge. I imagine if I could measure the distance between each of the twenty tie-dyed shirts on a hanger I would find that they are exactly one inch apart. Exactly.

Kaylee looks over at me and smiles.

I shrug. "I guess you don't worry about what you're going to wear in the morning," I joke.

Zorba doesn't hear me, or perhaps he doesn't think it's funny. He closes the closet and reaches for his rainbow-ribboned top hat instead.

"Ok then. Have you heard the story of the three bears?"

"Of course. Are you really going to tell us that story?"

"Patience, Boss. Just sit and listen, will ya."

"Ok," I say. Kaylee comes to sit beside me on the couch.

Zorba's rendition of The Three Bears is nothing like the fairytale we were told. It's a story that makes us laugh, and at times, even cry. Zorba is a master at weaving magic into everything. Kaylee and I never want to leave. We wonder at one point if the story will ever end.

When it does, Zorba removes his rainbow hat and bows. Kaylee and I clap and whistle and cheer, "Bravo, Zorba. Bravo."

"I think we need to go," Kaylee says out of the blue. The clock above the boat's kitchen sink says 4:30. Holy cow, we've been here for an hour and a half already.

Zorba stands and pulls his hat down around his ears. "Yes, yes. Don't be late. Come again. Do come again soon. I enjoy your company. You fill my cabin with goodness and fun. Come back before my boat sinks from the weight of all these lollipops."

Zorba bows again. His hat falls to the ground this time. We laugh. The giggles squirm inside the whole way home, and I feel alive. Happy almost.

PART II

The Sinker is an off-speed pitch that, when thrown, causes the ball to sink as it approaches the batter. The idea is to get the batter to swing over the ball and miss. When the people you are supposed to trust start throwing you sinkers, it's almost impossible to connect.

CHAPTER EIGHT

The first two weeks of our summer vacation were chewed up and spit out doing hard labor for Sea Trek.

Mom, Dad, and Harley arranged a punishment for us. I'm pretty sure it was mostly Mom who came up with the sentence. They called it restorative justice for breaking the rules and lying to Sea Trek and Mom. I called it hard labor, and a drag. Kaylee and I hauled kayaks from the water's edge to the racks across the beach all day for two weeks. We had to hose down life preservers, paddles, and kayaks in the scorching hot sun. The chilly bay waters were just inches away, but we weren't allowed to jump in to cool down. Once in a while, Kale and I would squirt each other with the hose, but if we did it too long, Harley would tell us to "knock it off and get back to work."

No one ever spoke about it again. The disappointment in Dad's eyes seems to have disappeared. But the sparkle never came back. I think about the words that Zorba planted in my mind. Maybe Dad's disappointment doesn't have anything to do with me. There's a bit of relief in that thought. I wish he could find the sparkle again.

I read somewhere that the universe is slowly dying as old stars fade faster than new ones are born. My family is the universe that my father is slowly fading away from.

Labor camp has ended. Today is our first day of summer camp. Hallafreakinluyah! It's bound to be an improvement.

"Hurry up, kiddo." Dad's been calling Kaylee away from the bathroom for the past ten minutes. She's gone into overtime at the mirror. Why do girls spend so much time growing their hair long just to strangle and hang it at the back of their head?

You should have heard Kaylee wail when Mom told us we were going to have to spend the summer in camp rather than between houses because our parents "couldn't trust us to make wise decisions on our own anymore."

As soon as Kaylee found out her friends Casie and Levi were going to be at camp, she started counting down the days until our Sea Trek sentence was over and Camp Rock Out began.

"Kaylee, will you get out of the bathroom. I'm going to pee all over the floor if you don't move. *Now!*"

She must have a crush on Levi. Why else would she be rearranging her hair for the fourteenth time?

"Hey Flip, Kaylee, come on in and get your pancakes. We're going to be late for your first day at Caaaaaaamp Rock Out!" Dad says Camp Rock Out as if he were practicing to be a cheerleader.

"Dad, give it a break," I plead, even though I know he'll do it more if he thinks it bugs us.

"Really, Flip? I was thinking I'd make a banner and hang it off the back of my truck. It'll say, 'Rollin' Like a Stone at Camp Rock Out.'"

See what I mean?

"Daaaad, don't you dare." Kaylee pushes past me and into the kitchen. I see Dad wink at her.

Steaming hot pancakes. Our favorite. When Mom and Dad were together, Dad was the one to make the pancakes. Mom says she made hers too chuffy and fluffy on purpose so that she could get a "long-deserved Sunday morning break." Now I guess she gets her long-deserved break every other Sunday.

Kaylee pours a ton of maple syrup over her pile of pancakes.

"Kaylee!" Dad yells. "Maple syrup is liquid gold. Eight dollars a bottle. Don't pour it like water please."

I wonder if that was a joke. A quick glance at his face tells me it wasn't. We hear it a lot these days. "No, we can't do that, it's too expensive," or "I'm not made of money, kids. You can wear those jeans a bit longer."

We finish our pile of pancakes in silence.

"I'll call you tonight to get the first day of camp report. I start a new job today. It's up north again so it might be late." I don't know whether to celebrate or cry. I know exactly what a new job up north means.

I know I shouldn't, but I ask anyways, "Can we come back next weekend?"

"It's your mom's weekend. She's going to want to do something fun with you." Kaylee snorts and some of her pancake goes up and out her nose.

"Ewww gross, Kale, that was crazy nasty." I jump back so she doesn't snot all over me.

"Tell me about it," she says. "I just got pancake up my nose." None of us mention why she was snorting, but we all know. Mom's working triple time now because Dad can't give her the money she needs to help with food and rent. I heard them fighting about it over the phone.

"Alrighty-o kids, pack it up, we're outta here."

In the wink of an eye, a lift of the voice, the mood shifts, and all is right in my father's world.

#

Camp Rock Out is on the sunnier side of Mill Valley. Even so, a bank of white fog hovers over the round edge of the hill when we get there. Some days the fog is like a solid ceiling that slowly presses in on me.

I'm too old for camp. Camp Rock Out has a baseball team for the older kids. Kaylee opted for the regular camp activities. Dad says camp is a way to keep kids safe and contained. He used to play kick ball and baseball in the local parks and back lanes of Connecticut where he grew up.

"Things have changed since then," he assures us.

Things have changed for Kaylee and me too. We lost our parents' trust. I miss Zorba. We haven't had any time to sneak away to see him. Our parents are determined to keep track of us all the time. Sometimes I think I hear him calling to us.

Kaylee hugs Dad and waves over her shoulder as she heads for the sixth-grade group. They stand in a cluster under a hand-painted sign. They look like they're waiting for rain the way they're huddled together.

"Love you, Dad."

"Love you too, Kale."

Dad waves to her and then turns to me. "Alright bud, I'll see you next Wednesday."

"*Next* Wednesday? What about *this* Wednesday?"

"I thought I told you this morning? I start a new job up north. It's going to be really hard to pick you up on Wednesdays. I won't be home until late. But we'll have two weekends in a row after that."

I imagine myself jumping up and down with pom poms in my hands – yippee, yahoo. Two weekends in a row.

Dad gives me a side hug and messes with my hair.

"Ok, Dad. See you." I pull away and walk towards the baseball field. I long for a familiar face in the small circle of kids on the field. There's none. I wish Ricki was here.

A few of the boys in the circle look my way and nod.

"Hey," says one tall, long-legged kid who reminds me of my good friend Kenny in the city.

"Hey," I say back.

"Welcome to the baseball division of Camp Strike Out." I offer up a smile for the joke. I stand and wait to see what's next.

123

There are two kids off to the side. I wonder why they don't join the group. One of them is a girl with a long blond ponytail dangling tight and high on her head. I can almost hear it pleading to be cut loose. The other kid with the short hair is wearing a camouflage hat, cargo khaki shorts, and a dark blue t-shirt. I'm not sure whether he's a she or a he.

One of the boys in the circle notices me looking at them. He leans in and says, "That's Amy and TJ. They're sixth graders. Don't let the girl in them fool you though, they're both better than most of us on the team."

"TJ's the one with the camo hat; she can out-hit just about everyone here," another boy adds.

"Yeah, and Amy is like a cheetah, she runs the bases so fast."

"Wow I've never played in a co-ed league," I tell the guy standing next to me.

One of the taller boys with really short blond hair snorts. "Ha, I would hardly call this a league," he looks at the others as though he expects them to laugh along with him. "It's more like a joke," he looks at me as if I'm the joke he's talking about. His stare hammers me behind the eyes. I'm relieved when he turns his back to talk with some of the other guys. A gust of cold air moves across the field and hits me like a slap in the face.

The guy who looks like Kenny asks, "So where you from? I've never seen you here before."

"I'm from San Francisco." I realize I'm not from San Francisco anymore. I don't feel like I'm from Sausalito either. I guess I could tell him I'm from Guatemala but that's way more information than I want to give.

"I live in Sausalito now. My family moved there from San Francisco a few months ago."

A short guy with shaggy red hair and a bright yellow t-shirt that says "Camp Rock Out" yells out from across the blacktop. "Let's head for the field players. Everyone here ready to play ball?"

He looks like he's old enough to be my dad. I guess he's our coach. I'm not impressed. His eyes find mine and he waves. "Hey, some new blood – great! I'm Carl."

"I'm Flip."

"All right. Like the name. You play ball during the year?"

"Yeah. I'm on the school team in Sausalito." God I hate being put on the spot. Could we please just go play ball now?

"Great, what position do you play?"

He shifts the huge sports bag from one shoulder to the other and I wonder if he has picked up the wrong bag and brought the one with bowling balls in it.

"First base, right field, and sometimes shortstop," I answer.

"Wow, you could be a team all by yourself," the blond-headed guy says.

The cold wind comes back around. It hits me on the other side of my face.

"Alright then, let's get started. Grab a ball and a glove if you don't have your own and let's practice."

I keep my eye on the blond guy. I think he's someone I will need to avoid. Amy comes up behind me. I almost whack her in the head with my glove as I take it out of my bag.

"Hey. I'm Amy, and this is TJ," she points to the girl with the camo cap beside her.

"Hi, I'm Flip. How ya doin?"

"It's not a joke," TJ says in almost a whisper. "The only 'joke' here is Steve. He's a really bad joke too." Amy is nodding in agreement but says nothing.

"Sorry?" I'm not sure what the heck she's talking about.

She looks over at the blond dude and jerks her head in his direction. "The jerk who said this is a joke."

"Oh, yeah. He seemed a little uptight." I feel like I need to be careful. I don't know who's friends with who, and I sure don't need to be making enemies the first day of camp.

"Most of the guys are cool, just ignore Steve. His brother's a jerk too. I guess it runs in the family," TJ adds.

I'm not sure how to respond. I just smile.

"Come on," she says, throwing one of the balls she'd taken from the sports bag. "You wanna throw with us?"

"Sure," I say. The other guys have paired up with one another.

#

The "Camp Strike Out" baseball team is relaxed. There's very little competition between the players. This feels like a vacation compared to Willow Tree Academy of No Team Spirit.

But I have other worries here. Steve seems obsessed with following my every move. Whenever I make a play, hit a home run, or catch a fly ball, I feel his eyes on me. Sometimes I hear him mutter under his breath, but I stay far enough away from him that I can't hear what he's saying.

Why does this guy hate me? I didn't date his sister and dump her or run his dog down with my bike. It's beyond weird.

Today we get off the field a little before lunch starts so I decide to head over to where Kaylee and Casie are playing kickball.

"Alright, Casie, kick it out of the park," Kaylee cheers her on. The ball comes rolling in for Casie to kick. She does. The ball goes sideways, hits one of her own teammates in the head, and lands back on the field.

"Fair ball," someone cries.

"Foul ball," someone else chimes in.

"Hard ball," yells the girl who was hit in the head, brushing her long brown hair from the side of her face.

This totally cracks me up. I stick around for a couple more kicks. Casie stands ready at the plate again. The ball comes rolling in with more bounce this time. Right before she kicks it, the same girl screams "Take cover," which cracks me up again.

Watching them play reminds me of when we used to play as a family. Kaylee would kick the ball off to the side almost every time, and Mom would jump up and down screaming for her to *run*. Dad would roll his eyes at me and remind them both that a ball kicked off to the side was a *foul ball*.

Suddenly it hits me. We will never play anything together as a family again. How can a family just break up and cease to play together? I twist my shoe into the hard surface of the blacktop.

The game breaks up, and we all head for the picnic tables together. I look around to see where Steve is sitting. He's nowhere in sight.

I sit down next to a kid I recognize from Willow Tree. I heard Levi call him Flynn. He's talking to Kaylee's heart-throb Levi. Actually, in all fairness, Kaylee hasn't said she has a crush on Levi, but sometimes you can just tell.

"What's up with the chilies? Your Mom's always putting them in your food, and you're always plucking them out?" Flynn asks Levi, who has just taken a bite of his cheese and turkey sandwich and plucked the chili peppers from the middle, putting them to the side of his napkin.

"It's her Mexican heritage," Levi says. "She just doesn't consider food edible if there isn't something in it to light your world on fire."

Mexican heritage? He looks about as Mexican as my little sister. He's got dirty blond hair and blue eyes. In fact, he looks more like Kaylee's brother than I do.

"Well, pass it on over here." Flynn holds his hand out and waits for the chili peppers. Levi gives him the chilies and watches as he puts them in his sandwich.

"Oh man, that's just wrong – chilies and tuna – no way, Flynn."

"Hey dude, don't yuck my yum." Kaylee cracks up. Maybe it's Flynn she has a crush on.

"I like your t-shirt, Flynn," Kaylee says.

I read the t-shirt. It says, "Some people are like clouds. When they go away, it's a brighter day."

"That is a good one," I say and then get up to leave. "See ya later, Kale."

I feel the warm breath down my neck before I realize it belongs to a person. The hot air whispers in my ear. "So you like hanging out with the girls, huh? Are the boys just a little bit too

128

rough for you? Or do you just feel more like a *tough guy* when you're with a bunch of girls?"

I don't even have to look to know who it is. I turn around anyways. Steve's ugly puss is right up close to the side of my face. I want to head-butt him. Something inside tells me he'll kill me if I do.

"That was my sister."

Fool.

Loser.

Butthead.

I keep those to myself, wishing I had the guts to say them out loud.

"Your sister? Yeah, right. I doubt it." And of course, I've forgotten that my dark brown and Kaylee's peachy tan summer skins do not say "brother and sister" to this moron who probably wouldn't get it even if I spelled it out for him. So I don't. I walk ahead faster and catch up to a couple other guys on the team. I zig-zag around them, putting Steve on one side and me on the other so I don't have to smell his stinking breath.

#

Dad cancelled our weekend together again. Mom tells us over dinner Friday night.

"I have to leave for work early today, kids. I have the opening shift. Flip, you need to pick up that room of yours, and Kaylee, I'd like you to do some summer reading." Mom organizes our day from the kitchen sink. I can feel the smile inching its way across Kaylee's face.

"Okay, Mom. Could we go downtown to get an ice cream later?" She sounds so innocent and pure. Girls get away with things when they do that. It's not fair, but I'm not unhappy about it now. Kaylee is buying us a ticket to Zorba.

"I suppose. But I want you to go there, get your ice cream, and come home. Is that clear?"

"Crystal clear," I say with a bit too much sarcasm. Mom's disapproval flashes like a warning flare across her face. "We'll come right home after we're done." I try to sound like a good boy even though our plans for disobedience are dancing a jig inside my head.

"Great. I'll be finished around five. Maybe we'll grab a burger or something when I'm done. I'll give you a call. We can meet at *Burgers by the Bay*."

"Sounds good, Mom." Kaylee smiles big now. That smile has nothing to do with hamburgers!

The minute Mom's car pulls out of the driveway, Kaylee comes into my room. She stands in the doorway and cups her hands around her mouth as if she was calling to someone far away. "Flip, are you in there? Should I send in a rescue helicopter? Or the firefighters, so they can cut a path to you through the forest of junk on the floor?"

"Oh, aren't you funny? Practicing for your audition on Comedy Central? You might want to go back to your room and work on your material a bit more. What you've got now isn't gonna leave them laughing!"

"Ok, whatever. How are you going to finish cleaning this room in time for us to go see Zorba?"

"Kaylee, it's only ten thirty. Mom doesn't want to meet until five. We have time to clean my room, read an entire book, and get an ice cream before we go to the docks. Chill, will you?"

"*We* aren't cleaning your room, Flip. *You* are! I'm going to do my summer reading; you are going to hire a steam shovel and a dumpster so that you can find your bedroom floor again."

Kaylee can be such a superior little twit sometimes. "That's fine, but think about it – if you helped, we'd be done that much faster."

"Someone has to stay near a phone in case we need to call in a search and rescue team to haul you out of there."

I laugh. Her material is improving. "Come back in four hours then."

Twenty minutes later, Kaylee's at my door. "Seriously, Flip? What have you done? It's still a mess in here."

She's right. Even I'm amazed at how much stuff there seems to be. My dirty laundry has reproduced like rabbits burrowing under my bed. My socks are scattered in so many places I can't find a matching pair. I also can't tell the clean laundry from the dirty. Mom has a nose that knows, and if I throw the clean laundry in the dirty laundry basket, she'll really have a hissy fit. She has a pet peeve about that.

"This is a big job, Kale."

Kaylee has no sympathy. She goes back to her room.

"Fine. Be that way." I pick up a shirt I'm pretty sure I wore to camp the other day. I give it a smell. Yep, it's a stinker. I hate this job.

She comes back thirty minutes later and lets out a long, slow whistle. "Wow, I'm impressed. Mom's going to find out if you dumped it all out your bedroom window, you know."

"Hey, how 'bout a little admiration and awe for a job well done?"

Before she has time to shower me with compliments, the phone rings. "I'll get it," Kaylee says as she's running down the hall.

"Oh, hi Mom. Yep. I just checked on Flip, he's still alive in there but I've got the Sausalito Fire Dept. on hold in case we need them to come in and dig him out. I know, right? Yes, I've almost finished the entire book. Ok. See you at five for dinner, Mom. Love you too. Bye."

"Whoa, that was lucky. What if she keeps calling to check on us?"

"I don't know. Let's leave right now. She won't call again for at least an hour, and then we can say we went for ice cream."

"Flip, I'm beginning to think this might be a bad idea. Do you know what Mom and Dad will do to us if they find out we lied again?"

"Well, we won't lie. We will go get an ice cream and walk along the docks on the way home. Can we help it if we meet up with Zorba along the way?"

Kaylee doesn't say anything. I know her need to see Zorba is going to win over her fear of getting in trouble. "Come on, let's get out of here."

Zorba's on the dock when we get there. He's doing something to the front of his boat. "Hi, Zorba. We've come to visit," Kaylee calls out.

"Yes, yes I know. Come along, I've been waiting. You're late, you know. We've got lots to see and little time. Come along, come along, come along."

"Uh oh, I think it might not be a good day," I whisper softly because I've learned Zorba has super-sonic hearing.

"I think every day is a good day with Zorba," Kaylee whispers back. "Where are we going, Zorba?"

"Well, funny you should ask, Princess Leah. Today we're going on a tour through time. A meander down memory lane. A hop down the rabbit hole, if you will. Are you ready?"

"Of course, we are," she says without a moment's hesitation. "Let's go."

I don't want to be the voice of reason just yet. I'm as curious as Kaylee about where we might be headed. Zorba unfolds himself from his crouched position. I swear he's wearing the exact same curtains Mom put up in our living room. I'm going to have to check and make sure they're still there when we get home. "Zorba, who makes your pants for you?"

"Well now, Boss, I think you're becoming psychic. Come along with me and I'll introduce you to my seamstress, my serpents, my mermaids. Some of them have gone to Davey Jones' Locker. Most of them, really. But not my beloved Belinda. She's made of material that never fades. She's the last of the lot, the only thread holding the tapestry together. Come along, come along on a magical mystery tour."

Zorba jumps in the air and then heads for the inside of his boat. His tie-dyed shirt is tucked neatly into the beige curtains he's wearing as pants. The wide cuffs at the bottom are a bright green shiny material that catches the light of the sun and glows. His red Vans with candy cane-striped laces peak out from beneath the glowing green. They remind me of Christmas.

"I can't wait to meet the woman who dresses Zorba. She's got to be someone special." Even though Zorba's inside his boat, I whisper.

"What's he doing in there? Is he going to leave us out here again and change his mind?"

"Here I am, here I am." On cue, he leaps onto the deck of his boat. He's got on his top hat now, and his black dinner jacket.

"Alrighty then. It's time for us to leave." We follow Zorba as he walks down the docks, away from the street. Three boats down from his own, he stops. "This is Margaret May I's boat. Of course, she's no longer there to ask if you may, but when she was, she was the gatekeeper. I couldn't make a move without asking Margaret May I for permission. 'Margaret, may I take the dinghy out on the Bay? Margaret, may I go to town to have a cone?' She made sure I never got lost and kept the child snatching protective people at bay. Without Margaret, may her soul dance and prance, I'd have been swept away from the Good Ship. She was my mother's best friend, sister, and keeper. But even she couldn't keep her safe. My mother didn't ask Margaret if she may. She just went on her merry way. She sold the anchor and went adrift. Now they're sailing the same seas together again. Off they've gone. Off they've gone."

Zorba doesn't look at either of us while he talks. He stares out beyond the brown shingled A frame boat with blue trim and geraniums all over its deck. I want to say something, but I'm afraid if I say the wrong thing, Zorba might change his mind about the magical mystery tour.

"And over here, across from Margaret May I, lived *Truancy Tim*. Monday through Friday, he'd come to take my hand and escort me to school. No matter how hard I'd kick and scream, Truancy Tim made me go. 'They'll take you away if you don't show up,' he'd warn."

"But Zorba, who slept on the Good Ship with you? Did you stay there all by yourself? You couldn't have."

Zorba stops moving. He's frozen in his shoes. I look over at Kaylee and frown. We stand completely still, afraid to stir the air around us in case the ripples disturb him.

Zorba takes off his hat and holds it out, as if he was begging for money. "Here now, my curious little kitten. Put all your questions here in my hat. This is a listening tour, not an ask questions one. That's it, take them all out of your mind and put them here in my hat. When I put it back on my head, your questions will rest atop my brain and I'll answer them all, one by one, when the time is right, not when it's wrong."

Kaylee tips her head as if she was spilling all her thoughts into her cupped hands. Leaning forward, she pours the empty air into Zorba's hat. He smiles at her, his eyes sparkling. I'm sure it's not real, but I can *feel* a warmth radiating off their bodies like a bridge between them. Zorba tilts his head and closes one eye. The open eye finds both of mine and I know it's my turn to tip my thoughts into his hat. I follow Kaylee's lead and pour the air into the hat.

"Well, I'd have thought you'd have a few more questions than none at all. Not to worry, Boss, your questions will be answered even if you keep them tucked away in your noggin'."

I have no doubt they will. None at all.

"And so, where was I? Ahh yes. Truancy Tim. Alright then. There's nothing more to say about him. He was a good uncle. A wise man who knew that books and chalkboards were necessary to grow a young boy's mind, expand his world, and keep him safe. Here, look here."

Zorba puts his hat back on his head and moves down the dock quickly. Kaylee and I follow. Two boats down on the opposite side of the dock is a purple boat with pink trim. It looks like something out of a fairytale.

Zorba takes his hat off again. He bows deeply in front of the boat. I'm not sure if we're supposed to do the same. Kaylee knows, though. She bows low along with Zorba. I follow her lead. It occurs to me that if the person who lives in this boat comes out his/her door and sees the three of us bowing in front of it, they might just call the police.

"Listen up, Tom and Jerry, this is the Good Ship's sister. She's as beautiful today as she was when I was a half pint. This is the home of the only Mermaid left me. Here's the answer to your question, Boss. Belinda the Beautiful lives here. Her doors are closed and her curtains drawn. That means she's not taking visitors today. But she's in there. Always home. Always there when I need her. She was my sister, my soul mate. We'd skip and play along these docks til her Pa would call us in for dinner. This is where I spent my time. Here on the Purple Palace. My boat was rented out til I was old enough to sail her myself. It was here with Belinda and her Pa that I did most of my growing. So, there it is. Both your questions asked and answered. Back to the Good Ship we go."

Zorba has a lollipop in the pocket of his dinner jacket. He tiptoes across the bridge from the dock to the Purple Palace's door and leaves the lollipop in a little basket nailed to the pink trim. Then he tiptoes off the boat and without a word leads us back to the Good Ship.

When we reach his boat, he turns to us. "Well now, my fine friends, the magical mystery tour has ended." He tips his hat and turns on his red sneakered feet. He doesn't look back. He closes the door to the Good Ship behind him and our visit has ended.

"Zorba, wait. Did we do something wrong?"

The window to the Good Ship pops open.

"Wrong? Do something wrong? You could never do wrong, Pocahontas. You are the essence of everything that's right. The magical mystery tour has ended because the Yellow Brick Road needs repairs. Come back again my friends. Please do come back again."

Zorba closes the window and that was that. I hate how unpredictable he can be—how he just calls the party to an end when he wants. "Come on, Kaylee, the Great Oz has spoken, again."

Kaylee doesn't move. She stands staring at the window, willing it to open again. She's not letting go.

"Kale, come on. He's had enough of us for today. We'll come back another time."

The window pops open. Zorba looks out at Kaylee and laughs. "Well now, My Little Engine that Could, you've come back again. All right then. Come on board and we'll have a cup of tea. The Mad Hatter is home and waiting for your company."

"I knew it," Kaylee says as she skips onto the Good Ship.

I wish I knew anything when it comes to Zorba. The magical mystery tour becomes a trip to Alice in Wonderland. I jump down the rabbit hole with Kaylee.

"So then, Boss, you've got some questions still swimming around. Not the serpent, mermaid type of questions, are they?

137

You're wondering what to do next. What move on the chess board of life you need to make in order to keep your king from being boxed in and taken down. Am I right?" Zorba has taken a seat on a stool with driftwood legs in the corner of the room. Above him is a large photo of a woman with beautiful long black hair. Her face so thin and her nose so sharp, she looks like a sliver of the person she's supposed to be. I wonder if it is Zorba's mother watching over him in the only way possible.

"I guess so." I should be shocked that Zorba knows what's going on in my life, but here on the Good Ship, "normal" has no meaning.

"Well, life's a tricky business. Keeping your king tucked away in a corner protected by the queen and the bishop isn't always the best move. The knight has ways of getting around the wall of safety without having to crash through. Sometimes, Boss, even if it looks like the worst move on the board, moving the king forward towards enemy lines is the most strategic move. You get my meaning?"

"I think so. You're saying I can't hide, that I have to step forward and face the enemy. Right?"

"Yes, yes, exactly. Outwit him. Listen and watch and you will know the right moment to step forward. Our enemies are sometimes our greatest teachers, you know. There's something to be learned from them. They help us grow."

I think about Steve and how tiring it is to have to keep track of him. I can't imagine what it is I'm supposed to learn from someone who goes out of his way to treat me like crap.

Kaylee shifts. Zorba jumps off his stool and comes towards me. Kaylee and I are still standing in the middle of the room. Zorba's arms are outstretched. He places his hands on my shoulders. His breath has a sweet candylike smell, and his words whisper into my ears. I'm not sure whether he's speaking them aloud or if they're streaming into my mind through his own. "When all is said and done, you'll understand how to find your way home in that bag of bones you inhabit, Boss."

Zorba smiles and winks. He throws his arms up into the air and spins in a circle. The next thing I know, he's holding Kaylee's hands and they are spinning in circles. The warmth of his hands still rests on my shoulders. It's the only way I can be certain that what just happened wasn't a dream.

"Come on, Boss, let your legs loose, feel your feet on the floor. Can you hear the music? Look at my little ballerina here, spinning to the sound of the flutes floating on the edges of the air. Join us, you need to move that bag of bones a bit so they can dance through the rough spots and rest like logs on a beach when the water's surface goes glassy. You get my meaning?"

His words make no sense and yet I *do* get their meaning somewhere beyond thought and reason. "Yes, Zorba. I think I do."

"That's the way. Now pick up your feet and move them to the beat of the music."

I find myself listening even harder for the music. My feet begin to move, they've found the rhythm that's hidden in the pockets of magic that float around the Good Ship Lollipop. Before I know it, my body is spinning and Kaylee has one of my hands, and Zorba the other. We're spinning in circles laughing.

Zorba begins to sing, "Ring around the rafters, pockets full of quarters, candy, lollipops we all fall down." He tugs on our hands and we all fall down in a heap on the floor.

Zorba sweeps his hands across the floor and scoops up something invisible. He holds it in his cupped hands, stands up, and throws it into the air. "You've got to give the music back to the gods or they won't have it for the next time you're ready to dance, don't you think, Boss?"

"That makes sense to me, Zorba."

"I knew it would. Now, who's ready for another story?"

"I am," Kaylee's arm is in the air waving frantically as though she had the answer to a favorite teacher's question.

The Good Ship Lollipop is a place where time gets lost. The air inside rises, falls, and swirls in such a way that time can't find a straight path from one minute to the next. Two hours becomes two minutes. Day becomes evening, but you have no sense of the sun's passing overhead when the doors and windows are closed.

Kaylee tucks her legs beneath her on the couch, and I sit on the floor with mine outstretched in front of me. Zorba takes us through the homes of the Three Little Pigs. One is made of baby's breath, soft and fragile. The next one's walls are a child's laughter, strong for as long as the laughter lasts. The third and strongest house is made from mother's love. Nothing can knock those walls down.

Zorba doesn't just tell a story, he becomes it. He's never still, always moving, painting pictures with his words as well as his body. It's better than any movie I've ever seen.

As his story comes to an end with a house made from a mother's love, Kaylee jumps from the couch and points to the clock on the wall.

"Oh crap." I spring from the floor, panic raking joy from the walls of my body at once.

"Have you gone AWOL my little truants?"

"What does that mean?" Kaylee is hopping in place, she's so nervous.

"Absent Without Official Leave, that's what AWOL means."

"Oh. Oh, yes. We are. Well, sort of. We have to go."

"Maybe we should go straight to the burger joint and just say we went early."

"I feel the rope tangling around your feet, Boss. Tangles and knots. Lots of knots. Watch your step. You could get snared."

"Okay, Zorba." I ignore his warnings. "I will. We need to go now."

"Goodbye, Zorba." Kaylee rushes towards him and wraps her arms around his waist. Her head only reaches his chest.

"Goodbye, Cinderella. Hurry home before your dress turns to ashes and your carriage becomes a ball and chain. Hurry, hurry home you go."

"Thanks, Zorba. We'll see you soon."

"Soon as the moon comes over the hill. Soon as the loon lands on the lake. Soon as soon can be."

Kaylee and I fly home. It occurs to me when we reach the house that Kaylee didn't ask me to slow down. Not once. I know it's not logical, but I'm certain Zorba has something to do with that. Seconds after we close the door behind us, the phone rings. It's Mom.

"Hello."

"Hi, Flip. You sound out of breath. Is everything okay there?"

I wait for her to ask us why we didn't answer the phone when she called throughout the day. "Everything's fine, Mom."

"I'm going to finish a bit earlier than I expected. My last client cancelled. Do you and your sister want to head towards town now, and I'll meet you at the burger joint for an early dinner?"

"Sure, Mom, that sounds great."

"Ok. I'll see you soon."

I hang the phone up and begin to laugh. At first, it's a slow rumble that rolls from my belly to my chest. But the moment it meets the air, it blasts its way out.

"What? What's so funny, Flip?"

"I don't know," I manage to say. "We have to go back into town to meet Mom early. Now. For some reason that seems funny."

I think I left the Good Ship with a part of Zorba sewed to my soul.

CHAPTER NINE

Staying away from Steve is a fulltime job. He waits for me around every corner. TJ and Amy notice it too. TJ says he focused on her the first year she started playing ball.

"He targets people who are different than him," she tells me. "He thinks that anyone who doesn't fit his idea of *normal* needs to be put in their place. I think he needs to get a personality myself."

I like TJ. She tells it like it is.

We're playing a friendly practice game today. I guess Steve didn't get the *friendly* part of the memo, though. He goes out of his way to find me and brush up against me as he comes in from the field. He's like a bad case of poison oak. No matter how much you scratch, the itch never goes away.

I think I hear him say, "Watch yourself, Speedy," but I can't be sure.

My cleats dig into the earth. I'm sure they're trying to dig a hole big enough for me to crawl into.

After a few quick outs, it's our turn at bat. TJ's up before me. She gets a good solid hit. I take my place at the plate. Steve is playing third base, and TJ is waiting for me on second, ready for me to send her home.

The pitch comes in. I get a good piece of it. The ball flies over the shortstop and drops out beyond the left fielder. TJ rounds third seconds before I tag second. The ball isn't in the air yet, I continue on towards third. TJ is on her way home.

Steve stands on the baseline waiting for the ball. Coach Carl yells, "The play is to home."

The outfielder gets the ball and throws it in to Steve who has a great shot at getting TJ out and preventing the run. Instead, he stands on the plate and waits for me to come into third. I don't see it coming. I figure he's going to make the play at home, so I keep running for third base at full speed. By the time I see that he's still got the ball, it's too late to stop. I try to slide but he's all over me.

The ball is in his hand, not his glove. When he tags me, he slams me full force with it. I hear my shin crack in two. Or at least that's what it feels like.

"Out!" Steve yells, looking over toward the designated third base coach. The coach nods and agrees.

"Out!" he says.

The guys on his team are screaming at him. The short stop yells, "Dude, the play was to home. You could've stopped the run."

Steve scowls at the player and then looks straight down at me and smiles. I'm brushing myself off trying not to show how much I'm hurting. Shooting pains are going up and down my leg.

"Yeah, but I liked the idea of getting Speedy Gonzales here out instead."

The shortstop shakes his head. I look at Steve. The hate I feel inside is like nothing I've ever known.

I force a smile and say, "Well, thanks for the run, that makes it two zip I believe." I trot down the white chalked line to home.

TJ gives me a high five, "Way to sacrifice for the team, Flip." The other players agree, and for the first time in a very long time, I feel like a part of a team. It makes the throbbing in my leg just a little less painful!

I work even harder at staying away from Steve for the rest of the day. When I get up from the table at lunch, I can feel my shin throb. I head for the bathroom. Under my pants leg, the bruise is dark, and the bump on my shin looks like a painted Easter egg.

"Idiot, jerk," I say, but it doesn't help with the pain. I wish I had some ice.

Later that night at Dad's when he asks about the game, I want to tell him what happened, but I'm embarrassed. I know it's not my fault, the way Steve feels about me. But I feel dirty all over.

Kaylee and Dad want to play Scrabble. I'm not in the mood. "I think I'm just going to go to bed," I tell them.

Kaylee looks at me funny. "Flip, it's only eight o'clock."

"Are you feeling alright, son? You've been so quiet all evening."

I look at my dad. His hair has gotten even lighter in the summer sun. It seems thin and transparent the way it hangs across his forehead. "I'm tired, Dad. We did a lot of running today at camp."

I head for the mattress in the corner of the room wishing that this place had bedrooms with doors that close.

#

There are dents in the couch cushions where Kaylee and I have spent most of our childhood since we moved to Sausalito.

If you asked me what was on the TV right now, I couldn't tell you. It's background noise. My thoughts are wrapped around images of Steve and how I'm going to avoid him.

Mom hollers from the kitchen. "Flip. Kaylee. Come take the garbage and recycling out, will you?"

I turn to Kale and sigh big time. "You do it," I tell her, but even I can feel there's not much push behind my command.

"She asked *both* of us, Flip." She huffs and gets off the couch, turning the TV off. She chucks the remote at me.

"Hey!" I pretend to be hurt but Kaylee's not buying it. She rolls her eyes at me and goes to the kitchen.

On the way to the green and grey buckets where we now get to color code our trash, Kaylee stumbles and drops the grocery bag full of garbage in the front yard. Globs of food and coffee grounds spill onto the fog-soaked lawn. Not only is Sausalito the loneliest place on the planet, it's the foggiest as well.

Kaylee has a fit. "Oh my god. You have got to be kidding me. What else is going to go wrong? This is the worst summer ever!" She starts to cry as she crams the spilled garbage back into the bag.

I wonder for a minute whose summer she's describing – mine or hers. I'm confused. Wasn't it a week or two ago that she was laughing and joking with her friends at camp? And now all of a sudden she's having the worst summer *ever?*

I drop my recycle bag with its nice clean paper, plastic and tin foil, and go to help Kaylee pick up the rest of the garbage on the lawn. "Kale, what's up? I thought you were having such a good time with everyone at camp."

"I am. Sort of. It's just a lot of work. I miss my friends in the city. I miss Dad."

The last time we saw him was the week before last. The Wednesday Steve split my shin in two. His new job has stolen him from us.

We finish picking up the garbage on the lawn, except the gross coffee grounds which I rub into the wet grass with my foot. I throw the garbage and the recycle all in one bucket and head back into the house with Kaylee. I wish I had something useful to say. I don't.

Dinner is something other than pasta for a change. The three of us work silently on our chicken and rice. Mom looks so tired she can barely lift her fork. She throws a weak conversation pitch to anyone who wants to take a swing at it. It lands with a plop. Kaylee and I are in the dumps.

I decide to throw Mom a line since she's trying so hard. "Did you ever read *Zorba the Greek*?"

"No, I never did. I saw the movie with your father. It's his all-time favorite."

"I bet the movie isn't as good as the book." I didn't mean for that to come out like a challenge, but it did.

Mom gives me one of those looks that comes from the corner of her eye because she doesn't turn her head the whole way around to face me. It's that look that says, "I'm not sure I want to be in this conversation with you, but I'm considering it."

She probably doesn't want to be in the conversation with me, but I don't realize that until the conversation has taken charge of my mouth and gone where it wants.

"Don't you think that's kind of strange? Don't you think that if *Zorba the Greek* is Dad's all-time favorite book that you should've at least read it? Maybe you could've gotten to know Dad even more, maybe there's stuff you just didn't understand about him because you didn't know him well enough. Did you ever wonder about that?"

Mom's looking at me now. Straight on. Eye to eye. Hers are squinting a little bit as if she needs to look very closely at me to be sure I'm who she thinks I am.

"*I think* you are moving into territory that is beyond your comprehension," she says. I can tell she's just winding up for a pitch that's going to come in slow and steady. "*I think* that my relationship with your father is not your business. And *I think* that I understood your father just fine, and reading *Zorba the Greek* was not going to change the things that were not working between us. *I think*, young man, that you should be very careful not to assume you understand what goes on between two adults in a relationship. You are thirteen years old and have no experience with what it takes to make a marriage work. Perhaps you should *wonder* about that just a bit."

I stare down at the chicken bones on my plate. There's still a little meat left on the leg bone, but not much. I feel a bit like that chicken leg right now. I'm sure if I peeked under my clothes I wouldn't be as fleshy as I was before that conversation about Zorba with Mom.

After dinner, Mom goes upstairs to rest while Kaylee and I clean up the kitchen.

"What the heck was that all about?" Kaylee asks me as we clear the table.

"Oh, forget it. It was a failed attempt at making conversation, that's all."

"I'll say."

Kaylee scrapes what's left of my rice and bones into the garbage. "Is something going on with you at camp?"

"What do you mean?" I pile the dishes one on top of the other with forks and knives sticking out from all sides. It's a daredevil tower that looks like it might come crashing down any second.

"That conversation you had with Zorba was weird. And I overheard Amy and TJ the other day talking about some guy who they thought might be a racist on the baseball team. It got me thinking about you. There are not that many kids of color there for him to be racist against."

I lift half the tower off the table and lower it into the sink. Not a single casualty. I haven't told anyone at home about the stuff with Steve. "Yeah, it's a snow white camp, that's for sure."

"I never really noticed until today."

I lean against the kitchen counter. "I guess you wouldn't notice. You're not the one walking around with a different color skin than most everyone around you."

She hands me another glass. "Was it you they were talking about?"

I start rinsing the plates one by one and think about Steve. "Probably."

Kaylee looks at me funny. I put the rinsed plates in the dishwasher. I turn around to look at her. What the hell, I think. I might as well just tell her. "There's something," my throat gets tight.

Kaylee looks at me and waits. Nothing comes out. "What do you mean, Flip? What something?"

My hands burrow into the thick of my hair, happy when they feel the flesh of my scalp. "There's this guy at camp. He's really out to get me. The other day on our way back from a walk into town for ice cream, a group of kids stopped in front of some workers doing sidewalk repair. The workers were all Latino. This guy, Steve, says, 'Look at this. Are we in Mexico or the United States?'"

Kaylee takes a seat at the kitchen table.

"The others didn't say anything at first. But Steve keeps talking. 'My dad says they're going to outnumber us soon.' Then he turns around and looks right at me. One of the other kids tells him that they aren't all Mexicans, but Steve doesn't seem to care. He goes on about how his dad says we Mexicans are going to take all the jobs and that they better start learning Spanish because pretty soon English won't be spoken in California. Then he looks at me and says, 'Hey Flip-ay' – trying to say my name with some kind of Spanish accent, 'Can you ask these guys in your language where they're from?'"

Kaylee's mouth is open wide. She raises her hands above her head. "Oh my god, Flip. What did you do? What a total scum puppy. Who is this guy?"

I don't want her to get upset. I don't want her to make a big deal of this. I knew I shouldn't have told her.

"You don't know him, Kale, neither do I, not well. He's not from our school. One of the other guys in the group got really mad at him, though, and told him to stop being such a jerk. I think Steve was embarrassed because he just turned away and mumbled, 'Whatever dude. I'm just saying.' Some of the other kids looked at me like they were sorry, and a couple just looked away like I wasn't there."

Kaylee pops up from the kitchen chair. "You have to tell Mom and Dad, or someone."

"*No!* I don't want to tell anyone right now, Kale. And don't you, either." I don't know why I feel so sure that Mom and Dad shouldn't know, but I do.

Kaylee picks at the skin around her fingernails. She looks up at me and says, "Let's go watch a movie, Flip, you want to?"

"Yeah, I guess so." I'm not really in the mood for TV but if it means we don't have to talk about Steve anymore, I'm okay.

I stand in the doorway of the den and think about Steve. I remember what TJ and Amy said about him always targeting someone at camp every year. I wonder why he does this. How does someone become such a jerk? I think about what Zorba told me – how I need to stop hiding and move towards the enemy. I can't imagine how or when I might do that, or even why.

"Okay, Flip?" Kaylee says loudly. "Earth to Flip, come in please. Can you hear me, Major Flip?"

"Yeah, yeah what?" I move into the den. Kale is turning the channels with the button on the TV – the remote has gone missing again. I quickly jump on the blue couch. My legs stretch from one end to the other. There's not an inch of room left for Kaylee to sit.

151

"I said, do you want to watch a movie or try to find something on the tube?"

Kaylee sees me stretched on the couch and rolls her eyes. "Oh, are you going to hog the *whole* couch? That is so uncool, Flip."

"Get over it, Sis. The couch is mine – my country, my ship, my kingdom, my castle. Mine, little sis, all mine." It feels good to mess with her.

"God Flip, you're such a lame dog. Fine, I'll sit on the floor while you lounge on the *only* comfortable piece of furniture in the room." She thumps down onto the floor at the foot of the couch.

"Sounds good to me," I tell her and then feel something underneath my rear. "And hey, check this out." I hold my hand up over my head. It's the remote.

"Yay. Sitting on it again? Jeez, Flip, didn't you even notice it underneath you?" She reaches up and grabs a pillow from the couch so she has something to lean on.

"Nope. No prince on a pea here. I could probably sit on a basketball and not notice it." I start to channel surf with the remote.

"I wouldn't brag about that, Flip, I'm not so sure what that says about you."

"Yeah, huh, you might be right about that. Numb butt. Not very brag-worthy, I suppose."

"Nope, I think not Captain Sleepy Cheeks."

The two of us start cracking up. I take another pillow from behind me and clobber Kaylee with it. We have an epic pillow fight.

The thought of Steve lingers like the smell of dead fish. I hold my breath and whack my sister over the head again.

"I need a dose of Zorba," I say and give her one last wallop with my pillow.

"Me too. Let's go tomorrow, Boss."

"Ok, Twinkle Toes."

#

We hear him before we reach the gate. His voice is a song and a shout. "Lollipops and raindrops. Sugar coated tears. Lollipops and raindrops. Sugar coated tears." He keeps saying it over and over.

Kaylee reaches the gate before me. "Oh no," she whispers. "He's having a *really* bad day, Flip."

I look at Zorba dressed in nothing but his top hat, rainbow scarf, and boxers. Zorba's in a place that's beyond day and night. He's left our world completely. "It looks a bit worse than that," I say.

Kaylee opens the gate and runs down the ramp. There's a small cluster of people standing on the dock, watching as Zorba throws handfuls of lollipops in the water, to the sky, and on the docks. The minute he sees Kaylee and me, he stops.

"There you are, there you are, Tweedle Dee and Tweedle Dum. You've come back. Here you go. Lollipops and raindrops. Sugar candied tears." He throws a lollipop first to Kaylee. She catches it. Then he throws one to me. It falls short and hits the deck. It lay cracked inside its clear cellophane wrapper on the dock.

"That's okay. Here's another, Boss." Zorba spins in a circle spraying lollipops as he goes.

Kaylee moves close to me. I feel her fear meet mine as she laces her fingers through my own. We walk a bit closer to the Good Ship.

"Come closer, Dorothy. Listen here, Boss, you're the Cowardly Lion. You need to find your courage. He's no different than the great Oz hiding behind his curtain playing the bully. Use your brains, Scarecrow." Zorba tips his head and closes his eye. His stare is laser sharp. It enters through the pupil of my eye. Steve flashes through my mind. He's small and frightened. He disappears.

"Here they come, bring in the troops. The fire brigade, the army. It's time to take old Zorba home," he says and looks over our heads.

I turn to see four paramedics and one policeman coming down the ramp. I get a sick feeling inside.

"Move aside, make way, folks. The cavalry is here. Come aboard men, it's alright. The Good Ship won't let you down." Zorba starts hopping from one foot to the other. He has on different colored socks, one blue, one white.

Kaylee sees the paramedics walk towards the boat and she's gone. She runs down the dock and across the ramp onto the Good Ship. Zorba stops hopping and looks at her.

"Hey kid, get off of there. It's not safe," the paramedics move quickly down the dock.

"Of course, it's safe. I'm not afraid. Zorba's my friend."

Zorba lets out a roar. It's laughter from so far down it doesn't sound human. Kaylee steps back. The paramedics come onto the boat. "Alright, Mr. Willis, we're going to take you with us," one of them says.

"You need a rest, Robin, we're here to help," says another.

"Leave him alone," Kaylee steps forward and takes Zorba's hand. He twirls her around as if she'd come to dance.

The paramedics look at one another. They're not sure what to do.

Zorba stops twirling Kaylee and bows. His top hat falls to the deck. "It's time now, my little mermaid, it's time for me to leave the stage." He let's go of her hand, but he doesn't stand.

One of the paramedics takes his arm gently, "Come on, Robin. Let's go."

Kaylee runs inside the Good Ship. She comes out with one of Zorba's tie-dyed shirts and the purple curtain pants with the gold trim. The ones he wore the first day we met him. "Wait," she calls out as she bends to pick up his hat. "He needs his clothes."

She moves towards Zorba and goes to hand him his clothes. He's standing up straight now, his arms to his side. He doesn't reach out to take them. The paramedics like bookends on either side of him take him away. He starts singing again, "Lollipops and raindrops. Sugar candied tears."

Kaylee stands hugging his clothes until the police officer takes them from her. "I'll be sure he gets them."

"I love you, Zorba," she cries. And then my sister crumbles in a heap onto the deck of the Good Ship Lollipop. She hugs her knees and sobs.

I run to her side and crouch beside her. "It's okay, Kale. He'll be okay."

The lady with the long blonde hair and the purple streak appears. She crouches down on the other side of Kaylee. "It's okay, buttercup, they're just going to give him some medicine to calm his mind. He'll be back. He always comes back."

"I don't want them to calm his mind," my sister sobs. "His mind is just fine the way it is."

CHAPTER TEN

The dark-haired kid looking back at me in the mirror today has a nose that is flat and wide. His teeth are short, almost square. His thick black hair is draped across his huge forehead.

The boy in the mirror doesn't look like the Cowardly Lion, but I feel him inside. I turn my back on him and grab my baseball cap off the toilet seat.

Mom and Kaylee are in the kitchen. Mom hasn't left for work yet.

"Morning, Flip. I'm making French toast for your sister, would you like a piece?"

"Sure. Thanks." Mom turns to look at me. I see none of myself in her pale moon face.

"You're up early this morning. Going somewhere?" I see Kaylee in her face. Not the eyes. Kaylee has our father's eyes. But her smile and even her pointy little nose looks just like Kaylee's.

"Yeah. Ricki called last night and invited me to hang out in the park and play catch for a while."

"Well, that's wonderful," she chirps all happy and excited as if I just told her I won front row seats to the Giant's game or something.

"No big deal, Mom. It's just catch. In the park. With Ricki." I go sit down next to Kaylee who knows better than to say anything to me right now. She sees that I'm slowly winding up for the kind of pitch that will bruise when delivered. She doesn't want to be the one to catch that ball as it flies from my mouth.

"Alright, Flip. No need to be snippy this early in the morning. I was just happy to hear that you've made a friend here in town, that's all."

Kaylee's eyes warn Mom, "you should just leave it alone," as they stare at her backside.

Mom scoops the French toast onto a plate beside the stove and turns to hand it to Kaylee. I search for more of Kaylee in the way our mother moves. She avoids eye contact with me and smiles at Kaylee as she puts the plate down on the table.

"You're up next, one or two?" There. There it is again. Something about the way her hand moves and she juts her hip out. Kale does that all the time.

"Two," I say. Two peas in a pod. Two people made up of the same genetic material.

Kaylee pours maple syrup generously over her French toast and digs in.

"Mmmmm." Melted butter and syrup drip from her fork. Kaylee's eyes close when she takes that first bite of French toast. They always do. So why does she look like a stranger to me right now? Why do they both look like people I've never met before?

I rub my hand around my neck and head. I'm exhausted. I hear a loud sigh and look towards Kale. Kaylee has mastered the art of looking at me without turning her head. I realize the sigh came from me.

Mom delivers my two pieces of French toast. There's a pool of butter melting in the middle of the top piece. I pour a ton of syrup into the pool and push the puddle of liquid around the bread.

"Okay, kids. That's it. I've got to get dressed and ready for work. I'll be back by four today. Flip, if you are going anywhere other than the park, be sure and call me so that I know where to find you if I need to."

"Okay, Mom," Kaylee and I say almost at the same time.

"Ahh, how nice," Mom smiles her Kaylee wide-open smile. "Compliance in stereo."

#

Ricki's waiting for me on the wall below the library and watching a game of basketball. I wave and head across the lawn. Oh my god! It's like walking on a sponge. I dance my way across.

"Tip toe through the tulips," Ricki sings as I squish and squash to meet him.

"Dang, that's like going through a freaking marsh it's so wet."

"Yeah, I don't think they thought that one through very well. Why water the grass right before the weekend when we all want to use it?" Ricki grabs his mitt and ball and jumps down from the wall. "Come with me, I know a place we can go that isn't wet."

"Okay." Whatever. I'm so glad to be hanging out with Ricki, we could be cleaning outhouses together and I'd be happy.

"How's Camp Rock Out?" Ricki asks, flashing me a smile. His smile looks familiar. Those teeth belong to the kid in the mirror this morning.

"It's not all bad." I stare at his teeth a little longer. I'm careful to look away before he wonders why I'm staring.

We turn onto a side street and up a steep hill. "Where the heck are you taking us?" I'm in pretty good shape but this hill is a killer.

"I thought we'd go to town and check out the ice cream place or the hamburger joint." He's got my tree trunk legs, thick and strong.

"Really? I just finished breakfast."

"Me too, but there's always room for a little more. We're growing boys, you know." He winks at me and gives me the kind of smile my dad does when we've just shared an inside joke.

"Well in that case, I guess we'd better go eat again. By the time we get up this mountain I will have worked up an appetite anyways."

Once we get to the top, I take a breather before answering Ricki's question about Camp Rock Out. "So there's this guy, Steve, at camp. He's been a total jerk to me since I got there, and I couldn't figure out why until the other day. I think he's a racist."

"Well, there are plenty of them to go around, especially here in Marin. People don't even realize they're racist here, but they are. What's this dude doing?"

"It isn't so much what he does as what he says."

Ricki nods, "Yeah, but did he come right out and say something racist, or is he just a *pendejo* who happens to have picked you to dislike?"

"*Pendejo?*"

"Jerk," Ricki translates.

I think about what Steve said, "Why don't you ask them in your language…" I'm not sure I really want to talk about all this. I can't seem to get the words to leave my mouth. Ricki turns his head as we walk and stares at me.

"Yeah, he's been pretty obvious about it," I say at last.

"Sometimes it's so subtle it makes you crazy. You think you're just imagining it." Ricki turns left at the top of the hill and continues. "When we go out as a family to some community function or to a restaurant, it isn't what the people say as much as how they look at us or speak to us. You probably don't experience it the same. Your family is white. Even though you're *Indígena*, when you're with your family, you're identified as one of them I bet."

"I guess. But I get the stares too. People are always noticing me when I'm with my family. The weird thing for me is that when I'm out in the world, I don't see myself as Latino. I forget what color I am until I'm in a place like Camp Rock Out, or when I look in the mirror."

"Yeah, your situation is definitely different than mine. But the racist stuff is going to be there no matter what color you see yourself as, because amigo, from where I'm standing here, you are as *moreno* as me, and that's *bien* brown!"

"What do you do? What do you say if someone talks crap to you?" I remember how stupid I felt when Steve was saying stuff in front of all the other kids. I didn't know what to say.

"Depends," Ricki says. "If it's big time racist – like calling you names or something – there's nothing you can say to someone like that, it'll just make it worse." Ricki stops and looks out towards the bay. I do the same.

"Whoa." I exhale loudly, still winded from the climb. The view is amazing. There are hundreds of boats in the harbor, and you can see Alcatraz from up here, and even San Francisco. "This is amazing."

"Yeah," Ricki says.

We stand quietly for a few minutes, then he turns and takes us to a windy road that leads into town. Before we hit the burger joint, Ricki stops in front of one of the touristy toy stores on the main drag. "Let's go in here for a minute. I want to get my little sister something for her birthday."

Once in the store, Ricki stands in the doorway for a moment. He heads for one of the aisles in the back. I follow him down the aisle and wait to see what he's after.

One of the women behind the register follows behind us and asks, "Can I help you boys with something?"

"No thanks, we're fine," I tell her.

Ricki says nothing and continues to stare at the shelf.

"Hey, whatchya looking for? It's nothing but tourist stuff here, dude."

Ricki seems to be concentrating on something and then looks up and smiles at someone behind me. I turn to see the same lady still standing there. She seems to be rearranging the shelves or something. I shrug and turn back to Ricki. I still don't know what the heck he's looking for cause now he's headed for the opposite end of the store down a different aisle.

"Dude, what are you looking for?"

I follow him down the next aisle. He's staring at a shelf of bobble heads. After a minute, he turns to me and nods his head in the direction of the other end of the aisle. I look. The same woman is standing there again, rearranging the shelves. I hear a bunch of laughing and see a group of kids at the other end of the store. Their parents are over by the cheesy card section with a thousand different shots of the Golden Gate Bridge. Ricki is still standing in front of the junk on the shelves. I get impatient.

"Come on, Ricki. Are you going to buy something or not?"

He shakes his head and says, "Nah. Let's go."

As we pass the woman arranging the shelves again, Ricki smiles big at her and says, "Have a nice day, ma'am."

She turns to him and smiles back, "You too, kids."

As soon as we walk out the door, Ricki stops and spins around. "Look," he says to me, nodding towards the inside of the store.

"Look at what?" I don't see anything.

"Where's the lady now?"

"Huh?"

"The lady that works there. Where is she now?"

I look inside and see her back at the register. Big deal. I'm missing the point big time here. "Yeah, so? She's working."

"Dang, you really *don't* get it, do you?"

"Get what?"

"The minute we walked through the door that woman noticed us. All the stereotypes she has saved up over the years

163

about Latinos being trouble started flashing through her mind." Ricki looks over at me to see if I'm following.

I'm following all right. He's got my full attention.

"So you and I start walking down the aisles. There are three or four other kids in the store, white kids. None of their parents are paying attention to them but no one seems to be concerned about that. But within seconds of our being there, she comes over and asks, 'Can I help you boys?'"

"So, what are you saying? She was following us? She thought we came there to steal because we're Latino? How can you know for sure? What if she was just trying to be helpful?" I feel afraid. Something about what Ricki is saying is messing with me.

Ricki rolls his eyes at me and sighs. "You're living in a bubble."

"Why?" I feel about two feet tall. "You can't know for certain that's what she was thinking."

"Maybe. But what I do know is that if you'd walked into that store with your family, that woman wouldn't have given you a second look because you'd have the advantage of having a white family to confuse the stereotype. Believe me, dude, that lady was not coming to offer us help because she thought we couldn't find what we were looking for on our own. Did you notice that even after you told her we were fine she seemed to need to reorganize the shelves in both of the aisles we were standing in? What a coincidence, no?"

I don't know why I can't wrap my head around this. Is it because my whole entire family is white, and I never thought I would ever be treated any differently than they would? "So the minute that woman saw us walk through the door, she said to herself, 'Uh-oh, two Latino boys, I better keep a close eye on them cause they're going to rob me blind?'"

Ricki shakes his head. "I honestly don't think she put it all together. That's what I'm saying, it can be subtle and sometimes people aren't even aware that they're doing it."

"How do you know so much about this?"

"I'm brown, dude. I'm brown in white America, and knowing it isn't a choice. I guess it helps that my father..." Ricki begins and then changes his mind. "What do you think my father does for a living?"

"I don't know – construction?"

Ricki shakes his head. "He teaches anthropology at the College of Marin. He talks about this stuff all the time. But I bet you didn't even consider that he had an academic job, right? Your mind went right to day labor. That's a form of stereotyping."

"I guess," I say, but I'm not so sure he's right. "But my dad is in construction, and he's not Latino."

"Hey, I'm not saying that only people of color are in construction. I'm just pointing out the possibility that in your head, you probably saw my dad as a laborer because you didn't have an image of a Latino man as a professional."

God, I think he's right. My head is spinning. I'm pissed now. "Let's go back in there. I want to see what she does if we go back in again."

"Nah dude, that's not a good idea. Of course she's going to wonder what we're doing if we come back in a second time. Come on, let's go get that burger."

I want to go back but I know he's right. I'm so full right now, I can't imagine trying to digest a burger.

CHAPTER ELEVEN

"Good morning." Mom's at the stove again. The only place I see my mother these days is over the sink, at the stove, or walking out the door. "How are you, Flip?"

She turns her back on the stove to look me in the eye. "I wonder if you'd like to have dinner with me tonight? Just the two of us."

I imagine sitting at the dinner table alone with Mom. A courtroom scene comes to mind. In it, I'm being cross examined by my mother. Her questions appear to be innocent, but they're designed to lead me into a world of self-incrimination.

I think about my shopping excursion with Ricki. There were no questions, or evidence of wrong doing. We were under suspicion simply because we were *shopping while brown*.

There's a gloppy popping sound coming from the stove. The oatmeal is bubbling. Mom whirls on her toes, the wooden spoon in her hand diving down into the pot of glop.

I think about the last few weeks at camp, the ways in which I've scurried around corners, or avoided standing next to Steve. Ricki's advice was to stay away from the obvious racists

166

because there's no point in trying to get them to see things differently. Zorba says I should go towards the enemy. I'm not sure who the enemy really is. And if the enemy is there to teach me something, is he really an enemy, or a friend?

I think of Zorba. I wonder what Mom would say if I told her Kaylee and I have been going to the docks and keeping company with a man whose craziness makes him the sanest person I know.

I wonder what Mom would say if I told her about what's been going on at Camp Rock Out. I wonder what she'd say if I told her I'm done cowering in fear of Steve. I imagine our dinner conversation would be very stimulating.

"Not tonight, Mom. I might be staying late at camp today. Maybe another night though."

#

Kaylee and I ride our bikes to camp. We've been doing that the last few weeks so that Mom can get to work on time. Kaylee's faster on her bike than she is on her feet, so I don't mind riding with her most of the time.

The bike path from Sausalito to Mill Valley runs along the Richardson Bay. There are dozens of snowy white egrets on the marshlands along the bay. Kaylee's beside herself with excitement. "That's twenty-three already and we've got a ways to go. How can there be so many of them in one place?"

I'm not in a chatty mood. I push my pedals a bit harder.

"I miss Zorba, Flip. When are we going to go see him again? He must be back by now."

"I dunno," I mumble. I have something other than white egrets and Zorba on my mind. I'm happy when we arrive and Kaylee runs off to be with her friends.

I stand at the bike racks for a few minutes. The air is full. It wraps itself around my entire body. It's the kind of full that presses in on you right before a storm. The sky is a calm, clear baby blue. Not a cloud in sight.

I spot the Monday morning Camp Rock Out groups on the field. Amy and Julius stand together. They're laughing. Steve stands so close behind them they could reach out and touch him. TJ is as far away from him as possible. She's talking with Kenny's look-alike, Zachary.

There's no hesitation. My feet do the thinking for me today. They make a steady march towards Amy and Julius.

"Hey Flip," Amy waves. Her strangled ponytail is split down the middle. Braids dangle on either side of the cloudy white sky of her face. Her cap has done its job protecting her from the sun.

He turns when she calls my name. The sight of me trips a switch in him. His face registers disgust. To be fair, the sight of Steve trips a switch in me as well. Normally it turns on an alarm and an urge to run the other way. Not today. Today my feet stand steady. My eyes lock onto him.

His blond hair is pasted dirty to his forehead. The sharp edges of his jaw follow a perfectly straight line to his chin. His nose rises from his face, a beacon of ethnicity and race. His blue eyes close in a squint – almost the way my dad's eyes do when he laughs. The similarity shakes my resolve just long enough that my locked eyes let loose and I look away.

Steve nods as if to say, "I thought so. Coward." He goes back to his conversation with Max. I try to engage his eyes again but he's lost interest.

"You look like you're ready to do battle," Amy laughs. I'm impressed with how well she's able to read me.

"Maybe I am," I say and look over towards Steve again. His hands are busy talking in time with his mouth. His smile is so big I could count his long white teeth if I wanted to. His t-shirt hangs out over his jeans the way mine would if I wore jeans. It's hard to believe that someone who looks so average could make my life such hell.

Coach Carl calls out from the blacktop, "Let's do it, team. We've got to get ready for the big game; we've still got lots of work to do." His small body lists to one side under the weight of his gym bag.

I wait. All day I wait for a comment, an insulting whisper in my ear, a shove from behind, something that will open the dark clouds and let the storm inside me loose.

Nothing. Not a word before lunch. Not a shove or a sneer on the field. Nothing. I want it so bad I can feel it where my shin used to ache.

"Say something," my mind calls out to him. "Say something so I can show you who I am."

#

On the bike ride home, Kaylee Chatterchops won't shut up about Flynn and Levi. "Levi's adopted, and Flynn's looking for his father."

I pedal harder. I hope the wind will fill my ears like cotton so I don't have to hear anymore.

"Flip, are you listening to me at all?" she whines from behind.

"I don't *care* about your *freaking friends*, or where they come from. *Just shut it.*"

The storm has broken. The thunder in my words takes the pedal power out of Kaylee's legs. The chatter clears like cloudy skies opening up to a sunny day.

#

Tuesday is Monday dressed in a new name.

Nothing happens. Steve has lost interest in me. I should be relieved. I'm not. The pressure in my head beats like a warrior's drum behind my eyes.

Kaylee doesn't ride home with me today. She's going on a bike ride with Casie. By the time she and Mom get home, I have shut myself in my room.

It doesn't help that my father called to say he wouldn't be able to pick us up again tomorrow. "I'm sorry, Flip. I promise I'll get you on Friday after camp."

"What happened to one week on and one week off, Dad? We were supposed to be doing that all summer. So far, we've had one week with you and a few lousy weekends."

"I'm sorry, Flip. I have to work. Things are tight, and this job..."

"Whatever," I shout. I'm not sure whether I pressed the "off" button before he had a chance to hear me though. He calls back. The phone rings three separate times. I slam my bedroom door and crank my music loud. Dad's favorite – Elton John, Yellow Brick Road fills the house, my room, and my head. *"You know you can't hold me forever. I didn't sign up for you. I'm not a present for your friends to open."*

He's a liar. A pretender. At least Steve shows his true self. I know what he thinks of me. My father promises me that I'm the most important person in his life out of the same mouth that tells me he doesn't have time for me. Again.

I reach for Zorba. I haven't opened it in the longest time. I turn to the page where Zorba's asking the Book Worm if he trusts him.

"Have you got confidence in me, Boss?" He asked, anxiously looking me in the eyes."

"Yes, Zorba," I replied. "Whatever you do, you can't go wrong. Even if you wanted to, you couldn't. You're like a lion shall we say, or a wolf. That kind of beast never behaves as if it were a sheep or a donkey: it is never untrue to its nature. And you, you're Zorba to the tips of your fingers."

I close the book. I know what I have to do.

#

Wednesday is dressed in fur and a lion's mane. It doesn't look anything like Monday or Tuesday.

On my way back to the field after lunch, I'm alone and alert. I can't tell you how, but I know it's going to happen. Soon.

I know he's there before I see him. His laughter crawls from the base of my spine up to the short hairs on my neck. I rake the laughter from my head. My nails cut deep into my scalp. The laughter continues. I know for certain it's directed at me. Wrapped like a present for his friend to open. I spin so quickly I almost lose my balance. He's only four long strides behind me. By the time I take my third step back, Steve has stopped laughing. His eyes aren't squinting, they're open wide.

"What are you laughing at, loser?" My words punch out at him. They aim for his face.

Steve steps back. His friend steps aside. I step forward. One step. Two steps. Three steps. Thump.

I didn't know I was going to do *that*. It wasn't the plan. In fact, I didn't have a plan past the list of things I wanted to say. But my fist had a plan. My fist has been aching to find a home in his flesh for weeks.

"What the...you crazy fool." He shoves me hard. Every place on my body was expecting a blow. I wasn't prepared to be shoved to the ground.

The steel-toed shoe that hits my leg is less of a surprise. It's the sister blow to the one planted on my shin a few weeks ago.

There's not time for me to get up and answer it with a blow of my own. Coach Carl has Steve by the arm. He looks like he may deliver my blow for me. I don't want him to. It's mine to deliver.

"He came at me. He hit me first. Ask anyone." Steve sounds like a scared little kid.

I stand up and step back just in case his foot decides to land a matching blow.

"Let's go, you two. We'll discuss this in the director's office when your parents get here to take you both home."

Steve walks on his left side. I'm on his right. He marches us into the Director's makeshift summer office.

"Sit," he says and points at two chairs on the opposite sides of the room.

"Ms. Litway, please call Simpson and Hathaway's parents. There's been a fight. I'd like them to come get their kids so we can discuss this with them."

Ms. Litway looks like she should be wearing glasses, she squints so hard looking for our phone numbers on her computer. She could've just asked us for our phone numbers. I wonder which of my parents she'll call. I don't have to wonder for long.

"Hello, Mrs. Simpson, this is Joy Litway from Camp Rock Out. Your son is fine, but you'll need to come pick him up. There's been a fight. We'll sort out the details when you get here." There's a pause. Ms. Litway's stern expression turns sour. "Well, that's fine, but please try to make it sooner if you can."

Mom's probably in between clients. She'll have to get another practitioner to take her next one. There goes forty dollars down the tubes. I'm dead.

Ms. Litway's pokey finger presses the numbers that win her a conversation with someone at Steve's house. I look across the room. Steve looks as if he's going to puke.

"Hello, Mr. Hathaway. Yes sir. I'm calling to ask you to come get your son. There's been a fight." She pauses and raises her voice just enough to make Steve shift in his chair as if she was speaking to him. "We can discuss it when you get here, Mr. Hathaway. We don't know all the details as of yet."

She says "as of yet" as if it were a threat.

"Fine sir, we'll see you then."

I rub my leg where Steve kicked me. I wonder if my punch hurt him at all.

Steve begins to babble. "Look, I don't know what his problem is. I was just talking to my friend and he turns around and decks me in the chest. I swear, I wasn't anywhere near him."

Ms. Litway doesn't lift her head. She peers over her imaginary pair of glasses, the ones that slide down the bridge of her nose and rest on the wide seat of her nostrils.

"We'll discuss it when your parents get here. For now, you can both sit there. Quietly. And wait."

I wonder what my mother will say. She'll probably just freak out about all the money she's losing because of me. I wish Ms. Litway had called Dad. But of course, he's in Santa Rosa. I hear him telling Ms Litway, "Much too far for me to come to Mill Valley in the middle of a work day," he'd say. "I'm sorry, I just can't manage it."

I'm sorry too. Sorry that I didn't get to say the things to Steve that I wanted. Sorry I don't feel the satisfaction I thought I would. Sorry that my father is more like the Book Worm than Zorba. Sorry about so many things in my stupid life I can't count them all.

I have a lot more time to feel Sorry in Ms. Litway's office. I'll spare you the list of ways that Sorry walks into the door of my mind and pummels me.

I glance over Steve's way to see if Sorry has landed anywhere near him. It looks to me like Sorry wasn't the visitor he was wishing would go away. Fear seems to have taken residence behind his eyes.

I watch as he finishes chewing the skin around each fingernail as if they are the last bits of meat on a spare rib. He looks down at the finger he's gnawed, probably to be sure there's still enough flesh left to cover the bone. Or maybe he's saving some for later.

His fingers are curled and cradled like a kitten in his lap when his father appears in the doorway to Ms. Litway's Office for Juvenile Delinquents.

Steve's father is Twin Tower tall. He wears a stiff white shirt and fancy pants with a crease down the center. His chest is so wide I wonder whether he's going to have to turn sideways to get into the room.

Coach Carl pops out from behind Hathaway's enormous building of a body. He looks like a very little person beside Steve's dad. He waits for Mr. Mammoth to move into the room before he scurries in like a mouse.

"Mr. Hathaway," Ms. Litway steps out from behind her desk. She has to tilt her head upwards to look into the eyes of Steve's skyscraper dad.

"Hello," his voice fills the room. Steve's kitten uncurls. His spare rib fingers are back in his mouth.

I watch as King Kong and Ms. Litway extend hands to meet in the middle. If he squeezes too hard, her fingers will fall off. Steve would probably love to make a meal of them.

His father turns to him. Fear is flapping its wings behind the whites of Steve's eyes. The kitten is back in his lap. "What's going on here, Steven?"

Steve's shoulders hop up towards his ears in a jittery shrug. "I dunno, Dad. I have no idea what this kid's problem is." Fear walks out his mouth with those words. It sits in his lap with the kitten.

Mr. Hathaway turns to look at me.

175

"Before we get into discussing what happened, and why, I'd like to wait for Flip's mother to arrive." Now that he's not peeking out from behind Mr. Hathaway, Coach Carl is back to his normal size.

"I have to get back to work so I hope that's going to be very soon," Steve's dad mutters.

#

There's a lot of light and space around Mom's body when she stands in the doorway about five minutes later.

"Mrs. Simpson, thank you for getting here so quickly."

Ms. Litway is once again out in the middle of the room, hand extended. Mom's hands are big in comparison to hers. Years of massaging have thickened her wrists and taken the delicate out of her fingers. I never noticed until now.

I feel her eyes on me. Mine are reluctant to meet hers, but they know better than to avoid them for long. "Flip, are you okay?" Mom asks.

I want her to be mad. The concern in her voice turns my frozen anger into a slush of little kid relief. I don't want it to. "Yeah. I'm fine," I try to bring my anger back to its big kid form.

Mr. Hathaway is not exactly subtle in his confusion about my coffee bean brown and my mother's cotton white skin. I can't worry about that right now. I'm in a world of trouble.

I decided the minute Steve's father walked into the room that I'm not going to rat him out. I don't want Mr. Hathaway, Coach Carl, Ms. Litway or our parents to stick their adult ideas and solutions between Steve and me. I need to finish this. It's mine. If I tell the adults in this room about the things Steve has said and done over the past three weeks, I know they'll want to rescue me.

I don't want to be rescued.

"Okay – let's get to the bottom of this and move on, could we?" It wasn't a request. Mr. Get-Out-of-My-Way is going to be directing everyone in the room.

I don't look away when he turns to me. I don't want to be reduced to a finger-chewing child beneath his oversized stare.

My dad says they're going to outnumber us soon. Steve's words find me right when I need them. I sit up in my chair and I dare Mr. Hathaway to stare at me a little longer.

Coach Carl steps forward. "I'd like to hear from the boys what happened. Flip?"

The room is filled with tension. My long silence threatens to bring it to its bursting point.

"Did you hear the question?" Mr. Hathaway punctures the silence. The air whooshes out of the room, and we all begin to breathe again.

"Mr. Hathaway, I'd prefer it if you let us address the boys." Ms. Litway has guts.

"The kid's not answering the question. In our home, when an adult asks a question you answer it. This kid needs to learn some manners."

My mother looks at Mr. Have-It-My-Way and in a voice I've never heard before says, "My son's manners are none of your business." My mother's got more guts than Ms. Litway.

"Please. Let's just try to find out the facts," Ms. Litway is pleading. "Flip, can you explain what happened, please?"

"I hit him." I look over at Steve.

He's waiting for the other shoe to drop. He's also probably waiting for his father's fist to nail him into the floor. Although my guess is that his father is probably proud of him for putting another *Mexican* in his place.

"Yes, we know that. But *why* did you hit him? Were you provoked in some way?"

"Hey – you're leading him on. Let him tell you why." It looks like Steve's father is a lawyer. Great!

"I hit him because I don't like him. He's a creep and he treats people like crap."

"Felipe!" My mother moves towards me. Mr. Hathaway nods his "see, I told you so" head up and down. "No manners," his smirky smile says.

"Steve," Ms. Litway turns to Steve. "You have a history of targeting certain people. Have you harassed Flip in any way?"

Is she serious? I'm quite sure Steve is not going to confess under the present circumstances. *Yes ma'am. In fact, I've assaulted Flip several times, used racist jabs and physical shoves as often as possible.*

Mr. Get-Out-of-My-Way bellows, "Wait a minute, here. This little boxer just told you he doesn't like my son and that he hit him because of that. I think we're done here."

Mom moves closer to me. I want to put my hand over her mouth. "Don't rescue me!" I scream at the top of my mind.

Mom looks at me. I think she's heard my silent plea because she nods at me. I swear I saw her nod. She turns back to Mr. Hathaway and smiles. She smiles!

Coach Carl rocks from one foot to the other. I almost feel sorry for him. "Flip, I've never seen you behave aggressively towards another camper. I find it very hard to believe that you would hit Steve without a more personal reason than the one you gave."

"*That's it*. If you are going to continue to pander to this kid, my son and I are leaving. There's some kind of reverse discrimination going on here and I'll have none of it. The kid admitted to hitting my son because he didn't like him. He needs to control his hot-blooded anger, and you need to stop looking for ways to blame my kid. Come on, Steven, we're leaving."

Mom puts a hand on my shoulder and nods again. I don't know what it is she sees, but I'm so grateful for her silence I could cry.

"Mr. Hathaway, I assure you there's no reverse discrimination going on here. Race has no part in this at all."

Too bad Ms. Litway has no idea what she's talking about. Race has everything to do with it.

"We're simply trying to get to the bottom of this." She turns to me. "Flip, violence of any kind is prohibited at Camp Rock Out. Because you have no history of aggressive behavior towards others, I am going to send you home today with a warning and a one-day suspension."

I nod.

"Steve, whether it was Flip who started the fight or not, you were seen shoving and kicking him on the ground. You too are suspended for one day. This is your last warning. If I hear of one more incident where you instigate or participate in aggression with another camper, you will be asked to leave and will not be able to return."

I want to laugh at this warning because I can't imagine Steve coming back here anyways. Camp Rock Out's baseball team only goes to seventh grade.

"Steve, let's go." Mr. Hathaway is clearly not happy. I watch Steve get out of his chair. Slowly. He stares at the floor. I want to see his baby blue eyes. I want him to know that this is not over.

I never get the chance. He follows his father out the door and doesn't look back.

#

Silence climbs into the car with Mom and me. It sits on the console between us.

Her car is clean compared to Dad's. There's always a wrench or hammer on the floor in the front seat of his pickup. I miss having to arrange my legs to fit around his tools.

The light is red. I feel Mom's eyes on me as she waits for the green. "I'm not going to ask you to tell me if you don't want to, Flip. I trust that whatever happened between you and that poor boy must have been serious enough to warrant your hitting him – if that's in fact what happened."

Silence jumps out the car window in a hurry. "*Poor Boy*? Are you kidding me? That *poor boy* is a racist thug. What are you talking about?"

"I'm sorry. I was thinking about what it must be like to have a father like that oversized gorilla. What do you mean, racist?"

I wish silence could've stayed a bit longer. I want to ask Mom to slow down in case it's running behind us and wants to jump back into the car.

"Never mind. I just don't think *poor* Steve Hathaway deserves your pity."

Silence must have wings because it's back on the console and stays there until we pull into the driveway of our nifty little home on Bayview Ave.

Mom turns the car off and twists her body in my direction. "Flip, I know you're angry with me for many reasons including some I don't think you even understand, but I want you to know this: I'm on your side. I may not approve of the choices you make all the time, but if you tell me the truth, I will listen, and I will help you work it out if I'm able."

I grab Silence by the tail and hold on tight. I don't want my mother to help me work this out. She can't. She has no experience with this. When my white mother walks into the Sausalito tourist shop, the woman behind the counter notices her for a nano-second. She sees white middle-class woman on the tickertape of her mind and goes back to counting money, or whatever it is she does behind that counter.

My mother can go into any store she wants and she doesn't have to consider whether or not the people around her think she's a thief or an illegal migrant worker.

My mother has what Ricki calls "white privilege." It's her ticket to everywhere and it's painted on her like a badge. She can't work the brown out of my skin. But the good news is – I don't want her to. And I don't need her help.

I let Silence go. "Thanks, Mom." I look her in the eyes. Both my parents have taught me the importance of looking a person in the eye when you speak to them. "It tells them they have your full attention."

I see how much my mother wants me to tell her more. The eyes may be the way to show someone you're fully there, but the flesh and furrow around the eyes lets them know what you're thinking. Right now, the waves of wrinkles above the shoreline of my mother's eyebrows plead with me to trust her.

I wish I could. I think after today I trust her a whole lot more. But I'm not ready to invite her in to this particular battle just yet. Zorba flashes across my mind.

"Thanks for not making me talk in the office, Mom."

"You're welcome."

"And by the way – you've got guts standing up to that Gorilla of a man."

"That man is a bully. If his son is a racist, it's because his father taught him to be. People learn to be racist, Flip. It's not something you're born to be. That boy has been pumped full of his father's rhetoric for years. That's what I meant by *poor boy*. He'd have to be crazy or braver than any child could be to stand up to the likes of that man!"

I see an image of Steve's spare rib fingers and curled kitten hands sitting in a nervous bundle on his lap. I want to hate him, but I know my mother's right.

"Maybe his dad taught him how to be a racist, but he learned to be an idiot creep on his own." I'm not ready to let *poor Steve* off the hook completely.

"Okay," Mom says. It's an okay that means – I don't necessarily agree but I'm not interested in hashing it out with you.

"I'm going for a walk," I tell Mom.

"Ok."

I've never been to see Zorba without Kaylee. I want to talk to him alone. I want him to laser eye a picture onto my brain that will tell me what my next move should be.

I walk onto the plank and board the Good Ship Lollipop. "Zorba? It's me. Are you there?"

I beg for the window to pop open, for Zorba's scarves and rainbow top hat to appear. I wait. I don't bother calling out again. Zorba has always known we were coming before we even arrive. I'm afraid he's not here. He's not coming back this time.

I go to the front of the Good Ship and I sit on one of the stumps. "Oh Zorba, what have they done to you?" The tears surprise me. I fold myself over my knees and I cry. "I need you, Zorba. Please, please come back."

"Hey there." I look up to see the blonde and her poodle standing on the dock. She's a bit like Zorba the way she pops into the picture. "He's home, probably just resting. I was just coming to check on him."

"Are you Belinda?" I ask, relieved to hear Zorba is home safe. The woman laughs down deep.

"He told you about my mother, did he?"

"Your mother? Is your mother Belinda?"

"Yes. She doesn't get out much. I'm Lydia. Did Robin tell you about my family?"

"Of course I did." Zorba's head pops out the side window. There's no top hat. His hair is neat and his eyes are still. "I could never leave you out of my life story, could I?" Zorba smiles and everything that was churning inside of me begins to settle.

"Zorba. I'm so glad you're back."

He closes the window and a minute later comes out onto the deck of the Good Ship. His legs aren't moving the way they usually do. They are stiff and heavy, they don't seem to be attached to the rest of his body.

"I'm back, but I'm only a shell of the man I was last time you saw me."

"Well now, Robin, let's remember, the last time this young lad saw you, you were heading off into the cosmos. Your feet are planted a bit more firmly on the ground now."

"Yes, yes. A barrel of medications will certainly keep one grounded like a boulder on a flat piece of earth. How are you, Boss? Have you found your way through the web of confusion that had you tied in little knots?"

"Excuse me, folks. I came to check on you, Robin. You look like you're doing just fine. I will leave you to catch up with your friend here."

"Goodbye, my sister. I'll see you soon." Zorba moves towards Lydia and they hug. He pulls a stump up next to mine and sits.

"I don't know, Zorba. It all exploded. I just lost my head and ended up in trouble. But I think I saw what you meant about our enemies being our teachers. I saw this guy who's been tormenting me for the past month and realized he's just a coward. I was giving him all the power, and in the end, he curled up like a kitten."

"Sounds like you figured it out, Boss. Now what? Where does it go from here?"

I was used to Zorba being able to see things without my telling him. I wanted *him* to look into the future and tell *me* what was next. It seems the medications have stolen his magic powers. The Zorba sitting next to me is just a regular guy, not the wild character Kaylee and I met before. I wonder if it makes him any less special to me now. As I think about this, a picture flashes across my mind. Zorba is dancing and waving his scarves above his head. He's saying something, but I can't quite hear. I listen harder. And then I do. *You're almost there, Boss. He's waiting for you, at the end of the Yellow Brick Road.*

I look up at Zorba. He sits quietly. His eyes are vacant and his mouth only slightly open. There's no wild left, no sparkling eyes or laughter bursting from down deep. But I'm certain he just reached out to me, in the way that he does.

"I guess I'll just have to see, Zorba. I don't know which way it's going to go. I know I have more I need to learn from this guy. It's not over yet."

Zorba nods. "Yep. I'm pretty sure you're right about that, Boss. There's always more to learn. The question is who we're supposed to be learning it from." He gets up slowly from his stump and his feet shuffle across the deck. I wait for him to say something. "Goodbye" or "I'll be right back." Something. But he doesn't. He walks slowly to the door and then turns and smiles.

"See you soon, Zorba. Kaylee will be really glad to know you're back. She missed you too."

Zorba's smile isn't the same as before, but I still feel the strength of it squeeze my heart and I swear it skips a beat. The door closes behind him. I sit for a few minutes longer before I head home. I feel safe here with Zorba.

Another picture flashes across the screen of my mind. My dad standing across from me in the park, his hand held high ready to catch the ball I've thrown in the air, waiting with his cock-eyed grin. I miss him. I miss my dad so much it takes my breath away.

I stand and look towards the window. It stays closed. I head home, eager to let Kaylee know that Zorba is back. He's not the same on the outside, but he's in there. I'm certain of that.

#

On Friday, Amy approaches before I reach the others. "Steve's been kicked out of camp." Her words are doing somersaults of joy, she's so excited.

"What?" I say. "How? Why?"

"Seriously, Flip? He deserved whatever you gave him. I'm sorry I missed it."

"We both got suspended. He didn't get kicked out." Panic rises and wraps its fingers around my throat.

"Did you really think they were going to let him stay here after the things he said to you? Coach Carl started talking to some of the others. They told him what they'd been hearing. I had no idea he was doing that stuff to you, Flip."

Oh god. Does everyone know? There were only a few guys there, how did everyone find out? I want to crawl into my sports bag and zip myself inside of it.

"Who kicked him out?"

"I don't know. All we know is that he's not here, and the word is he's out!"

"Forever? Or just the rest of the week?"

"Forever. Jeeze, you don't seem all that happy, dude. I thought you'd be dancing in your cleats with the news." Amy's annoyed.

"Yeah, I know. I should be totally psyched. I'm just shocked." The other kids are watching us. I need to look happy that Steve is gone.

"Whatever," Amy says and heads back to the group.

Coach arrives just as I'm about to turn around and walk off the field. I need to get out of here, away from everyone. I wish Ricki was here. He's the only one who might understand what's happening inside of me right now.

Oh crap, Coach is headed right for me. "Hey Flip, can we talk for just a sec?"

Can I say no? Do I have a choice?

He looks at the others on the field and says, "Okay guys, start warming up. Come on, get out there and get those gloves on."

"Take a walk with me son."

We walk out towards the eucalyptus trees that wind around the rim of the field. It's not foggy today, but I feel cold, way down deep. I wait. Coach says nothing for the longest time.

"How long? How long was the racist stuff going on, Flip?"

God, he sounds like he's mad at me. Seriously? "I don't know, awhile I guess." I feel small.

He runs his fingers through his hair, pulling it back away from his face as he does. It flops right back down. "Why didn't you come to us, son? Why didn't you tell someone what was going on?"

I wish I could answer that question. I don't know why. I know that something about the way Steve saw me even more than how he treated me made me feel ashamed. I didn't want to tell because I didn't want anyone else to see what he saw in me.

Coach stops walking and waits for an answer. I avoid his eyes. I don't want him to look into mine. I don't want him to see inside of me.

"We would have stopped it, you know. We don't tolerate racism here, Flip. You know that, don't you?"

It's not your battle, I think. I feel something strong inside of me begin to stand. *It's not your fight to fight. I don't want you to think that you can fix it, because you can't. It's not yours to fix.*

I say, "Yes sir. I know."

"He won't be coming back. He's been asked to leave, and he'll not be coming back to this camp again." He sounds so proud.

I feel deflated and lost. I don't want him to be gone. I want him to come back. I'm certain Steve has the answers to so many of my questions.

"I heard," I say, turning towards the field where the others are pretending to practice, but are really watching us. "The others told you what he said?"

"Yes. The kids were disgusted with what was going on, Flip. You should know that. I'd like to bring this up with the group. I think it's an important lesson."

What? Is he going to stand me in front of the group and talk about racism? You've got to be joking. "I'd really rather not, Coach. Can't we just leave it now? Everyone knows what he did, and they know he's gone because of it. You said it yourself, they were disgusted with him."

He stands quietly for too long. "Okay Flip. I understand. Let's go back and play ball."

I'd like to just go home now, but if I do, everyone will talk about me. "Okay Coach. Thanks."

He puts his arm around my shoulders and turns us in the direction of the field. I don't like the feel of his arm around me. It doesn't belong there.

At the end of the day, I find one of the guys Steve hangs out with standing by the bike rack. Without thinking about it, I approach him. He sees me coming and turns away. I don't care. I walk around to the other side of the rack. "Hey," I say loud enough that he can't ignore me.

"Hey. What's up?" I'm not sure but it seems like the guy's embarrassed. He's not hostile, but he doesn't want to talk to me either.

"I need to know where Steve lives. I need to talk to him."

"Seriously? That seems like a bad idea."

"Maybe, but it's my bad idea. Where does he live?" I stare at him. I'm sure it's not a bad idea, but I couldn't explain why if you asked me to.

"He lives over on Rosemont. Up the hill, in one of those houses with a huge wall around it and a locked iron gate." He looks at me as if he's trying to understand why I'm asking. "You can't even get in without the code, you know."

I didn't know. Damn it.

"Why would you want to talk to him? After all the crap he said to you? The guy's a jerk, why waste your time?"

"Well you seemed to waste plenty of your time hanging out with him." I stare at him hard. I don't see the person standing in front of me alone. I see him standing beside Steve.

He turns his body slightly away from my own. I think he's going to walk away. He shrugs and looks down. "I don't know why I hang out with him. I guess because it seems smarter to hang with him than to stand against him."

"Stand against him?" I must be shouting because the dude steps back a bit. "I never stood against him, beside him, or anywhere near him. The guy hitched his horse to my back side and rode me no matter how hard I tried to steer clear of him. He's like a reoccurring nightmare haunting you all day long!"

I take a breath and try to calm myself. In a flash, I see Zorba's smile. He nods at me and whispers, *Keep your feet on the Yellow Brick Road, Boss.*

What does that even mean? I stand quietly, hoping Zorba will fill the silence in my head with something useful. He doesn't. "What did he have against me? Other than the color of my skin, which clearly didn't work for him, why did he target me?"

"Because he's a coward. You were new. Just like TJ, you're different. You stand to get more attention than him. I don't know how his mind works. He doesn't talk about why; he just goes right in to trying to mobilize people to stand with him."

"Yeah, well he's a whack job. What's your excuse? You see all that and you still hang out with him. What does that make you?"

The guy's eyes lock with mine. I wait for him to blast me. I'm surprised when he says in a whisper, "A bigger coward than him."

I want to agree with him, but I see his shame. The ice around my heart cracks, and all at once I see my father's crooked smile. I wonder what he would say in this moment.

How would he deal with this guy? The question that comes out of my mouth surprises me.

"What's your name?"

"Oliver."

"Okay."

I turn to walk away. Oliver calls out to me, "He's a jerk for the things he said to you. I'm glad you decked him. I'm glad he's gone."

"Yeah, well maybe you shouldn't be. Maybe you need him around so you can learn how to stand up for yourself. I'm not glad he's gone."

Oliver freezes, then his head bobs in short little nods. "You may be right about that."

"Yeah. Maybe I am." I turn and walk away. The desire to talk to Steve is gone. I have nothing to say to him, nothing to prove. I realize standing up to him is almost like standing beside him. I'd rather just step aside and let him walk as far away from me as possible.

CHAPTER TWELVE

"I like your outfit, kid. I'm sure those socks are going to help Flip hit a whopping huge home run today at the Camp Rock Out summer baseball bash!" Dad's arms are spread open wide as if he is announcing the beginning of the World Series.

Kaylee rolls her eyes. She's got on her favorite overalls and her socks with the days of the week written along the rim. She's wearing them inside out for good luck. Today's the end of the summer game. I've got a good feeling about it. Dad hasn't missed a single Wednesday since my fight with Steve.

Kaylee and I have spent the last two weeks at his house. I have a hunch that Mom told Dad that my fight with Steve was my way of "crying out for help" and that he'd better start "showing up" before it's too late.

"Now remember, son, keep your head down, your feet solid and your eye on the ball. And be sure to get in front of that ball when it's coming at you on the ground."

"I know, Dad! You'd think I was going out for little league the way you're talking to me. This is my third year playing ball. I know how to catch a grounder. Jeesh."

"Alrighty, you about ready, Kaylee?"

Dad's putting his hat on backwards. Kaylee spins hers around to match. Mine's already there.

"Been ready for days, Dad. Just waiting for you two goof balls!" She jumps up off the couch and heads for the door. "Let's go do this thing," she says, trying to sound like Dad and me.

Dad and I look at each other and roll our eyes.

"So who's in the lineup, son?" Dad takes his eyes off the road to look at me. We're almost to the field in Mill Valley.

"Dad, what difference does it make? These are mostly Mill Valley kids – we hardly know any of them anyways."

"Okay then, scratch that question."

"Is Mom going to meet us there at the beginning of the game? Does anybody know?" Kaylee asks.

"She told me she'd be there no later than the first inning. She just had a couple of things she needed to take care of. She'll be there, honey, don't worry." Not only has Dad been "showing up" more, but he and Mom made a secret pact to show up together for birthdays and apparently baseball games.

"Oh man, this field has a hot dog stand! Awesome."

Kaylee jumps out of the truck and points over to where everyone is standing around with popcorn, popsicles, and hot dogs. We both look at Dad at the exact same time. He smiles, reaches into his pocket, pulls out a ten-dollar bill, and holds it out for us. I grab it first and wave it in Kale's face. "Whoever gets there first gets to spend it," I say and take off before she has time to think.

As the game is about to begin, I look over at the bleachers just as Mom arrives. Wow, she actually made it to my game on time!

We're playing the "Summer Slammers." My team, the "Roaring Rock Outs," are at bat. The Slammers' pitcher is warming up on the mound. Our first batter is Wynn. He's so thin he has to run around in the shower to get wet.

"Play ball!" The umpire yells. The game is on, and the chatter begins. "Atta boy, Wynn, show 'em what you got. Base hit, buddy, base hit." The pitcher winds up and lets his first pitch go.

"Ball one," the ump calls out. "High and outside."

The next pitch comes in, and Wynn swings the bat hard, so hard that when it hits nothing but air, his follow-through spins him like a top. That's okay. Wynn's a good hitter. Just watch when he gets a piece of that ball.

The next pitch comes in. He swings, and the crack of the ball on his bat is music to our ears. We're all screaming. The ball flies past the pitcher and drops behind the shortstop. "Run, run!"

Wynn may look like he's too thin to hold the bat up, but his long legs fly him to first right before the ball gets there. "Safe!" the first base ump cries. I turn to TJ and give her a high five.

Next up is Kernus. He's the only other kid of color on our team. "Alright, Kernus, bring him around, bring him around. You can do it."

The first two pitches are balls. The third pitch comes in a little high but Kernus likes it. He pulls back and connects. It's sailing up and into left field. Kernus runs as fast as he can, and so does Wynn. The left fielder snags it, but Wynn flies back to first just in time.

"Out. Safe." The ump cries almost at the same time. We groan and cheer.

The third batter is TJ. "Come on, TJ," I hear Kaylee screaming from the bleachers. Mom and Dad are sitting with Kale in between them.

The first pitch comes in a perfect strike. TJ stands like a statue. She doesn't move a muscle. It looks as though she's forgotten why she's even up at bat. We're all quiet. We know what to expect from TJ.

The next pitch comes in. It's a ball. TJ still hasn't moved. The next pitch is perfect – across the plate, waist high. TJ doesn't move. None of us do. Coach is standing quietly outside the dugout looking confident and calm. The pitcher looks nervous. He seems confused, as though he doesn't know what to make of this kid at bat who doesn't seem interested in swinging at all.

The fourth pitch is perfect. TJ moves, ever so slightly, shifting her weight onto her back leg just a little and we all know. She swings, connects and sends the ball flying. She slides into second right as the ball comes in from center field. Everyone in the bleachers stands up.

I'm up. Wynn's on third, TJ's on second. I spin my hat around so that it fits under the helmet and pull the helmet down over my head. I love the feeling of my head squeezed in tight.

I grab my bat and turn again towards the bleachers. Kaylee gives me the thumbs-up sign. Mom is clutching her stomach, and Dad just nods. "You've got this son." I hear his words, like so many other times, in my head.

I stand and stare the pitcher down. I look right into his eyes. And wait. The pitch comes in. A little low and inside but the ump calls it a strike. That's okay. I wasn't going to swing anyways. I'm just watching the pitcher. I want to see what he's got.

The next pitch comes in fast. I swing and miss. I don't look over at the bleachers. Now I'm in the game, full on. Me, the ball and my bat.

"Strike two," the umpire calls out. I feel a tiny lurch in my gut. I take a breath, I'm good. I've got this.

The next one's coming in slower. I can tell it's mine. I dig my foot in deep and send it sailing. The sound of the ball against my bat is like a gun at the starting line of a race. I throw my bat and run. I'm not watching the ball, I'm just keeping my eye on first base. I already know where that ball's going.

"HOME RUN!" The umpire yells. "THAT'S A HOME RUN!" I run like my life depends on it. Like it matters. I catch up to TJ who's just rounding third. I hear the screaming and see everyone jumping, and dancing, slapping first Wynn, then TJ as they cross home plate. I'm only a few steps behind her. The thumps on my back come in, one right after the other.

I turn quickly to see Kaylee and Mom both jumping up and down, screaming at the top of their lungs. Dad has his fist up in the air and his eyes on me at home plate.

#

We kicked their butts – seven to two. I hit another home run in the last inning and got on base every time. TJ kept the pitcher confused with her statue stance and got on base every time too.

Dad grabs me and pulls me in close, whacking me on the back. "Stupendous, outrageous, just the stuff the pros are made of."

After all the slapping and celebrating, Dad gives Kale and me a few more bucks to go get something else to drink. "You should've seen Mom. First, I thought she was going to die from nervousness, then I thought she was going to have a heart attack from excitement." Kale is electric, she's so excited.

"Yeah, I saw her clutching her belly when I came up to bat. Maybe that's why she doesn't come to my games. They make her too nervous!"

"That's exactly what she said, Flip!! Right after she grabbed her stomach and looked like she was going to puke, she said, 'Oh god, this is why I don't come to these games.' I told her to have some confidence."

We grab our drinks and move away from the line. I look over towards Mom and Dad and stop. Kaylee looks over too and asks, "How could they be fighting? They were just so happy just two seconds ago. What could they have found to fight about?" She looks over at me like I have the answer to her question.

Our mother's hands are whipping the air, short slaps here and there. She's chewing Dad out about something – that much is obvious. They don't see us as we walk towards them. We're close enough for me to hear Mom say, "It's time. You can't keep putting it off until..." and then she stops talking when she sees us.

Dad's face goes from looking like he's just been tortured to Bozo the clown with a smile so big and so fake, it makes me want to punch him. "Okay kiddos, how about a celebratory dinner? You in?"

A tornado inside of me spins months of hurt and anger into a funnel of fury and hurls it my father's way. *"No!* Enough. Just stop it."

Kaylee moves towards Mom and Dad. All three of them stare at me. But it's what my mother does that surprises me most. She nods. That same nod she nodded in the office with Steve and his father. I feel the nod like a hand on my shoulder. The tornado's spin slows.

"What are you talking about, Flip?" I don't look at my father. I need to gauge his words through my mother's actions. Mom's nod turns into an almost imperceptible shake of her head. It says "no."

Her "no" is like a musical note that is a pitch perfect match to the one that just blew out of my mouth seconds ago. The tornado inside of me ceases. I'm empty inside. All the hope and glory of this day is piled like debris in a heap at the bottom of my soul.

I look at my father. When did his movie star handsome become average good-looking? Where did the sparkle in his blue eyes go? His strong construction worker's hands look like Steve's curled kittens grown into cats.

It's not only the hope and the glory of the day in that pile of debris. I'm there too at the top of the pile. The little boy who saw nothing but sparkle and shine. He's twisted and torn. His body is draped over the debris like a tarp. "I'm tired. I'm ready to go home now," I say.

I look at my mother. I'm not ready to see my father in the dull light of the day.

"Yeah, me too." Kaylee says, looking at me, not Dad. "We'll see you next weekend. School starts in a few days and we have to get our stuff together."

"Seriously guys? Aren't we going to celebrate the big win? Come on, son," he begs. I wonder if his fingers will turn to spare ribs.

"Leave it, Fenton. The kids have school on Monday. We need to go home and get ready for that."

"Bye, Dad. See you on Wednesday, right?" Kaylee tries to sound as if everything is normal. Just like Dad.

"Yep. See you on Wednesday. It was a great game, son." He moves towards me with his arms open. I let him hug me, and then I turn to follow Mom and Kaylee.

CHAPTER THIRTEEN

I haven't spoken to Dad since the game last Friday. He missed our Wednesday for the first time in weeks. The new school year has started. The good news is that Ricki and I have several classes together. I guess you're wondering what the bad news is. There's no bad news yet. I just know there will be. There always is. There's no sparkle and shine to keep me from seeing the world as it is; I see things with a clarity so sharp it hurts.

Kaylee and Casie are in the same seventh grade class along with Levi and Flynn. She couldn't be happier. Kaylee still has a few layers of gauze over her eyes. I'm glad for her. I don't want to be the one to rip it off. I don't want to pretend, either. I'm glad she has some friends to hang out with now.

"Flip, your dad's on the phone. Pick it up downstairs will you, dear?"

Mom and I have found a new place of peace. She's so much cooler than I ever realized. Just one more thing I'm able to see more clearly.

I'm ready to talk to Dad. I trip over my sneakers on the way out of my room. I pick up the phone. "Hey Dad."

"Hello, Flip. How are you, son? I'm sorry about last Wednesday. There's a lot going on. In fact, I wondered if I could pick you up after school tomorrow and take you out for pizza or something? I want to talk to you."

"Talk to me? Uh oh, what's up, Dad?"

"No, son, there's nothing wrong. Actually, I've got some really good news. I just wanted to tell you in person." The great pretender has inserted himself into our conversation. I don't like it.

"Why don't you just tell me now, Dad? If it's good news, I'd rather not wait." There's a long silence on the other end of the phone. I see my dad winding up for the pitch. He's either going to throw a curveball or something more straightforward, like a fastball – over the plate and true. I pray for the fastball. Even if it comes in too fast for me to connect – I want it.

"All right, son. I found a job, a really good job that could last quite a long time. It's a huge condo complex that will employ tons of people and probably last over a year. It'll be fairly good money and it will be stable." He stops there. It was his slow ball. It came in over the plate nice and easy. I wait for the next one. Here it comes.

"The bad news is that the job is up north, past Novato in Santa Rosa. The money's much better than what I'm making now. But it's still not enough." It's a sinker. It started to come in straight, and then dropped down at the last minute.

I see the next pitch before it leaves his hand. He pauses a little longer and then delivers. "I'm going to have to move to San Rafael, buddy." There it is. A fastball right across the plate.

I don't know if relief and dread can take residence in the same body at the same time, but I'm pretty sure they just did.

I want to ask him how long he's known. I want to scream that this isn't the way things were supposed to turn out. He was supposed to live with me, in the same house, and be my hero, my superstar Dad, until I'm old enough not to need him to be.

He's supposed to protect you and rescue you? an older, newer version of myself asks.

I take a breath. I hold the phone away from my mouth and exhale long and loud. Then I bring it back to my ear in time to hear my dad asking, "Flip, are you still there?"

"Yes, Dad. I'm here. I heard you."

My father is moving to San Rafael. This may mean I will see him even less than I already do. But my father pitched me a fastball. Straight and true. He trusted that I could handle it. So I do.

"What does that mean for us, Dad? How will you come get us on Wednesdays? And get us back to school on Monday mornings?" I have to ask.

"I haven't worked out all the details, Flip. I'm sure we'll be able to work something out, though." I hear the familiar *it's all going to work out* tone in his voice. I let it go. He threw me a pitch and it was straight and true. That's what I've been hoping for.

I know now who I'm supposed to meet at the end of the Yellow Brick Road. It's not Steve, or Zorba, or even my dad. It's me. I'm the person at the end of the road I'm supposed to meet. Zorba's words come back to me. "Remember Boss, life's a tricky business. You've got to trust someone along the way until you trust yourself just enough to go it alone."

AFTERWARD

"Kaylee, over here." Ricki darts around me, his hands held high in the air. Kaylee throws the basketball as hard as she can right into Ricki's outstretched hands. I'm all over him, like flies on poo – blocking and bumping him as he nudges his way to the basket. Jayla, Ricki's sister, grabs his shirt.

"Foul!" Kaylee yells out. "You can't hold his shirt, Jayla." Jayla lets go. With a spin and a jump, Ricki shoots the ball into the basket.

"That's it," Ricki sings out triumphantly. "We win, twenty to twelve. Skunked you!" He high fives Kaylee and slaps me on the shoulder.

"Nice game, *amigo*, maybe next time!" We move off the court. A new group of players takes our place.

"You guys want to come to our house for a while?" I ask, wiping the sweat that's stinging my eyes. I'm not used to these hot days in San Rafael. The temperature difference can be as much as twenty degrees between San Rafael and Sausalito.

"No dude, we have to get home. *Es el cumpleaño de mi madre*, and we have to get dinner ready and eat cake!"

"Is today her actual birthday or are you just celebrating cause it's Saturday?" Kaylee wonders. I'm impressed that she understood Ricki, since she's only had a little Spanish.

"Today's the real day of her birthday," Jayla nods. Her bright purple headband shifts down towards her eyes just a bit. She pulls it off with a swift yank and brushes her thick black hair back with the palm of her hand. "Maybe I'll bring a piece of the *tres leches* cake to school tomorrow. It's the best!"

Kaylee smiles. She and Jayla have become friends since we're spending more time with Dad and riding back and forth to and from school with Ricki and her.

"Okay guys, see you tomorrow." Kale and I turn to head home. "Tell your mom we said, *Felize Cumpleaños.*"

Ricki gives me the thumbs-up sign. "Nice accent, Felipe. It gets better every day."

Kaylee nods in agreement. Jayla points to her and says, "You're next, *amiga.*"

"Hey, I'm practicing all the time. I have Señor Bravo for Spanish this year and he's hard core. Homework every night and dialogues in class every week. I'm gonna catch up to you guys in no time flat, you'll see."

On the way home, Kaylee and I go to the One Slice pizza place, and then walk down 4th Street. I stop in front the awesome display window at Triumph's. Skateboards and hand painted sneakers are propped up on tables and mini-fridges.

"I want to go see Zorba," Kaylee says. I told Kaylee about my last visit with Zorba. I also told her how his medication has taken some of the wild and crazy out of him. I don't think my telling can prepare her for the change.

"Yeah, me too. Let's go see him after school on Monday."

Kaylee nods and smiles. "Who creates these window displays? I love this store."

"I love this city," I say and keep walking. San Rafael *is* like the Mission District. I've come home again.

"Me too." Kaylee pops the last bite of pizza into her mouth and licks her fingers. I look over at my sister. I'm still not used to seeing her dressed in shorts and a t-shirt. She decided that seventh grade is the year to shed her "overall skin."

Funny, because this is the year that I decided to fully own the color of my skin. I am Guatemalan born, a Mayan of the K'iche'. I know now that being brown in this country means I have to be aware of the ways in which I will be treated differently, unfairly. I'm ready. I don't need to be protected or rescued. I just need people to be straight with me.

"You want to play a game of Battleship when we get home?" Kaylee asks, looking up at me with a grin. "Unless of course you're scared to. I did beat you pretty pitifully last time." She elbows me gently and adds, "And, I guess I skunked you in basketball as well. Not such a lame little sister after all, huh?"

I take off my baseball cap and whack her lightly over the head. "*Suerte, mi hermana.* Nothing but luck!"

Made in the USA
Columbia, SC
22 May 2018